• *Mixed Emotions* •

He stared at her for a long terrifying moment, and then he crossed the space between them and crushed her to him. He kissed the breath from her body. When he released her mouth, her knees had given way. But she found herself, inexplicably, caught up in his arms. He crossed the room to the divan, where he gently put her down, then settled himself beside her.

This gentleness of his confused her. He was looking so concerned, like a man who really cared about his wife. Was he going to react as he had that night in the carriage? She turned in his arms till she could see his face. "You are not angry with me?"

He dropped a kiss on her forehead. "I am outraged," he said, but his expression belied his words.

Jove Books by Nina Porter

Design For Love

Nina Porter

J

JOVE BOOKS, NEW YORK

DESIGN FOR LOVE

A Jove Book / published by arrangement with
the author

PRINTING HISTORY
Jove edition / November 1990

ISBN: 0-515-10442-6

Jove Books are published by The Berkley Publishing Group,
200 Madison Avenue, New York, New York 10016.
The name "JOVE" and the "J" logo
are trademarks belonging to Jove Publications, Inc.

PRINTED IN THE UNITED STATES OF AMERICA

10 9 8 7 6 5 4 3 2 1

For Mike and Pat
with love

Design For Love

• *One* •

SPRING HAD COME to England. Hedgerows were fragrant with bloom and the meadows seemed to have greened overnight. In the backland groves little leaf buds slowly unfolded and crowds of unseen daffodils thrust golden trumpets toward the sky.

But Robert, Earl of Dreyford, was not impressed by spring. Nor by the undoubtedly expensive garden in the formal style of Capability Brown that lay before his jaded gaze.

The earl had just driven cross-country. His closed curricle was of the newest and most comfortable design, so he wasn't tired. But he was exceedingly irked. The fact that the whole debacle was due to his own lack of foresight did nothing to mitigate his anger. And he was further irritated by the knowledge that he had made such a trip at the whim of a fat mushroom.

Dreyford took a calming pinch of snuff, automatically flicking his wrist in the proper manner. With graceful ease he replaced the snuffbox in his paislied ivory waistcoat and adjusted his coat of superfine. He was well aware that his tall, lean form was shown to advantage by his fawn inexpressibles and still gleaming Hessians. He was also pleasantly aware that though Charles Hinckley's clothing had obviously cost plenty of blunt, they only served to make the merchant look fatter and greasier.

The earl sniffed, perhaps a little louder than was necessary, and his green eyes grew icy. The Dreyfords disliked being trifled with. The present earl had only deigned to undertake this journey because of a particular piece of Irish land that had long eluded him.

But he was not the sort to marry for land. He was not the sort to marry at all. The earl's face darkened and the thrust of his chin and his hawk-like nose grew more pronounced. His eyes rested on the formal greenery outside the window, but it was *her* he was seeing.

The laughing green eyes, the mop of curling red hair, the freckles on her pert nose. He had felt for Katie Howard all the passion of a boy fast becoming a man. And his love had been returned, in all innocence, until that day long ago when death had snatched her away.

The earl straightened the broad shoulders under his well-fitted coat. Any hope of his marrying had died with Katie Howard, as many a hopeful mother had since learned to her disappointment. For him, as for his long-dead parents, marriage meant love. And there would never be another Katie.

It was not that he disliked women. *Au contraire.* In his three and thirty years he had known many women. And he had used them well. But, as he would be the first to admit, *use* was the appropriate word.

To none of these women had he vouchsafed even a glimpse of his soul. For none of them had he felt even a start of tenderness. He treated them well because he was a man of honor. But he did not love. He had learned early that love meant too much pain.

He turned to face Hinckley, noting again how the beady eyes sunk in the corpulent cheeks gave the man the look of a fat boar. A small smile tugged at the earl's thin lips. Hogarth could have made quite a caricature of the merchant. Stuck on a spit, with an apple in his mouth, turning over a slow fire. In his present mood, the earl found such a picture very gratifying.

"So, milord. What do you think?"

Hinckley's oily voice irritated Dreyford only slightly less than the merchant's annoying habit of rubbing his fat hands across his even fatter middle.

"I think you have bungled this matter badly," the earl said. He narrowed his gaze and Hinckley's pink face paled. "Any person in London could have told you that I do not take kindly to tricks."

"Tricks, milord?" Hinckley seemed genuinely surprised. "There are no tricks here. This is a matter of business, pure and simple."

Dreyford's expression darkened and Hinckley took a step backward. Tales of the legendary Dreyford temper had evidently reached his ears.

"You brought me here under false pretenses,"

said the earl, in a tone that even his peers feared. "You offered me a piece of land that is not yours to dispose of."

"Indeed, milord," replied the distraught Hinckley. "That is not . . . exactly right. That is, I *am* Cousin Fiona's guardian. And as such I am entitled to choose her husband."

Dreyford felt a twinge of regret for the unknown girl. With Hinckley as guardian she was devoutly to be pitied. "That may be so. But that man will not be me."

"Now, now, milord." Hinckley was all aflutter. "Just give the matter a little thought."

"I don't need . . ."

But the merchant had already bustled to the bellpull. "I'll just call the girl in, milord. Give you a look at her. After all, you've come this far."

Common sense and breeding kept Dreyford from voicing the string of curses that rose to his lips. It was abominable that for all his power as a peer he couldn't enact a law to rid England of such parasites. But he enjoined himself to a little more patience. No amount of distaste should cause him to descend to Hinckley's level.

Out in the garden, the object of their conversation sat unsuspecting. Fiona Byrne glanced at her charge, sitting beneath the budding linden tree. She should have insisted on a parasol for the fair-skinned Constance. Freckles were easily induced by too much exposure, and with Constance's wedding scheduled for the day after tomorrow, she must take care.

Fiona pushed back a tendril of gleaming auburn

hair that had escaped its severe knot. For herself, she relished the sun's warmth. Darkened skin and freckles across her nose meant little to a poor relation. A sigh rose to her throat, but she swallowed it silently. Constance was young for marriage. But Cousin Charles would not thank his poor relation for saying so. Of course, she would never have been so unwise as to voice an opinion.

Still, though Constance was young, perhaps this wedding was the best thing for her. The Viscount Garston was a good man—a trifle dull to Fiona's way of thinking, but essentially good. And he cared for Constance. That single fact did a great deal to elevate him in Fiona's opinion.

Cousin Charles was an avid social climber. Fiona was convinced that, had it been possible, he would cheerfully have sold his daughter to the highest bidder. Fortunately for her, Constance was not a raving beauty. Her features and her character were both too bland for even her father to have conceived of her capturing the ton's admiration. Garson, however, seemed captivated by her. And he had money and a title, thus satisfying Cousin Charles.

Fiona sighed. She was glad for Constance's happiness, but it did not bode well for her own future. Fear quickened in her breast and her hands nervously clutched the material of her plain brown gown. Lately Cousin Charles had been making ominous remarks about her lack of usefulness after Constance's departure. She had so few alternatives. Without references she could not hope for another position as governess-companion. Yet little else was open to a young woman of principle. If only. . . .

Her thoughts flew back in memory to the brief golden days of happiness when Lonigan had first come into her life. Dear fair-haired Lonigan had the lilt of the Emerald Isle on his tongue and the fire of love in his bright blue eyes. At sixteen she'd been unable to resist such a cheerful, loving man, whose kisses held her spellbound and whose promises of a golden future had raised hope in a heart long buried under despair.

So strong had been his hold on her, that mad wild Irishman, that even now, some seven years later, she could remember the feel of his hot kisses and his strong arms. The rest she had tried hard to forget. To recall those long nights of joy after their runaway marriage was too agonizing. Or the torment of his disappearance and the long days of searching and not finding, of watching her supply of coins grow ever smaller until it had dwindled to nothing.

With her money gone she'd had but two options: become a woman of the streets or return to Cousin Charles in abject humility. She had chosen the latter course. The life of a prostitute, though appalling, would perhaps have been easier to bear. But in the beginning she had fortified herself with the thought that Lonigan would know where to find her when he returned. And by the time that hope had faded she had become inured to Charles's sneers at her "sham" marriage.

But the lascivious gleam in his eyes was another matter. Though the death of his wife had given Fiona some fearful moments, she had come to see that as long as his daughter was in the house, she could hold herself reasonably safe. But now, with Constance married off, there would be no one to stand between her and the gross bulk of her cousin and guardian.

Though the sun still shone brightly, Fiona felt her skin prickle with gooseflesh. London's streets looked ever better. But how would she accomplish the journey, stranded as she was without a copper to call her own?

"Fiona! You're not listening to me."

Fiona forced a smile. "Yes, my dear. I fear I was doing a bit of woolgathering." Her glance went to Constance's white forehead, now puckered. "Don't frown," she cautioned automatically. "It causes wrinkles."

Constance dutifully relaxed the muscles of her face. But the moment she began to talk, the wrinkles returned. "I can't help it, Fiona. I don't know why Papa wouldn't listen to me. I do so want you at my wedding."

"No doubt he felt it was not proper," Fiona said, trying to soothe the girl. She never criticized Charles to his daughter. Her private opinion was that he was too pinchpenny to buy her a new gown and too vain to allow her to appear without one. This was also a convenient way to remind her, if such a thing should be necessary, of how dependent she was on his charity. Added to that was the fact that a new gown might be sold if she chose to run away, a prospect that she considered with increasing favor as the day of the wedding drew closer.

She was fully aware that running away would put her in a precarious situation, but she found that just about anything would be preferable to Cousin Charles.

"But I want you to be there," Constance replied petulantly, her pale face growing even paler. "I know I shall do something absolutely stupid, like falling over my gown."

"Nonsense." Fiona's smile was affectionate. "You know how much the viscount loves you. The rest doesn't matter."

"But if I pull some bird-brained stunt and disgrace Papa, he will be so angry." Constance's lips quivered at the thought of her father's wrath.

"Constance, my dear." Fiona was used to soothing her charge. She did it almost without thinking. "You are forgetting. After the ceremony your father will no longer have charge of you. You will have a husband then."

Constance brightened and the hands she had been wringing relaxed. "Oh, Fiona, that's right! You are such a blessing to me. If only Papa had seen fit to let you come with us. Everything would be top-of-the-trees then."

Fiona kept a smile on her face, though her stomach clenched. She knew why Charles had refused to let her go. And the viscount, no matter how he might wish to please his bride, could not be expected to intercede in this matter. "Those newly wed are best left to themselves," she said softly, aware that the excuse was flimsy, that there would still be a house full of other servants. "They need time alone."

"Yes, Fiona, but—" Constance's rejoinder was interrupted by the butler's appearance.

"Yes, Yates?"

"Mr. Hinckley wants you in the library, Miss Fiona. Immediately." The old butler's eyes were sympathetic. He most probably had some inkling of the unpleasantness that lay in store for her.

"Thank you, Yates." She turned to Constance. "Perhaps you had better go in, too, my dear. Too much sun is not good for your complexion."

She left her charge inside the door and made her way toward the library. As an impressionable child she had thought this big house full of statues and paintings a marvel of beauty. Now she was old enough to recognize ostentation. This was the house of a nouveau riche cit, a mushroom, as the aristocracy would say. But, ostentatious or not, Cousin Charles thought it perfect. And in her present situation Fiona had best appear to think so too.

Outside the library door Fiona pushed back the tendrils of hair that insisted on curling around her face. She paused only to lick her dry lips and square her shoulders. There was little point in delaying the inevitable.

Cousin Charles sat behind the great desk of polished oak, his corpulency exaggerated by the tight fashionable clothes he affected. "Come in, my dear," he purred.

"Yates said you wished to see me." Fiona hesitated a few paces inside the door. Her cousin's friendly greeting halted her more effectively than did his usual scowl.

"Quite right," said Cousin Charles with false cordiality. "Come in, Fiona, and take a chair."

Never in the long years that she had suffered under his care had she been invited to take a chair in this room. This was where she stood on trembling limbs, waiting for punishment to come. It was punishment she expected now, though she had no idea for what. Tentatively she looked around for a chair further removed from his desk. It was then she saw the stranger.

He stood near the window, somewhat back and to the side, which was why she had not seen him on entering. He was taller than Charles, whose height was considerable. But this man had no need for creaking stays to conceal unconcealable rolls of fat. The stranger was a lean man, wiry and spare. Broad shoulders and narrow hips gave him the look of a sportsman, and his elegantly clad frame spoke of strength as well as substance. A hawklike nose presided over a wide mouth grimly shut above a determined chin. His hair was black as polished jet and black brows bushed below it like fierce little hedgerows.

But it was his eyes that held her mesmerized. Green they were, like her own. And yet unlike. For she had looked in the glass often enough to know that her own were flecked with warm brown. But this man's were hard and cold as winter ice.

Though he maintained his outward calm, Dreyford's heart was pounding. She had the same bright hair, the same green eyes, the same freckles on the bridge of her nose.

He experienced the strangest sensation, as though Gentleman Jim Jackson had penetrated his defenses and dealt him a punishing blow to the solar plexus.

She was not Katie, of course. His mind knew that almost as soon as it registered the resemblance and it stopped him before he could move toward her. But he had suffered a severe shock to his nervous system.

This was not Katie. This was Hinckley's poor relation. She was clad in a gown of cheap bombazine that had obviously seen better days, many of them. Her rich auburn hair had been confined in a severe knot at the back of her head. That could not, however, hide its deep sheen, nor the beauty of a heart-shaped face that held jade-green eyes.

With a moue of annoyance, the earl recalled propriety and bowed his head slightly in greeting.

Fiona managed to acknowledge this with a nod of her own, but her teeth bit sharply into her bottom lip as she fought the sensation that this man was looking into her very soul. She swallowed the exclamation that rose in her throat, but she could not stop the flush that spread upward to her cheeks.

"Fiona. Sit down." Cousin Charles's voice finally penetrated her thoughts.

Startled, she tore her gaze from the stranger and advanced to the chair her cousin had indicated. She did not realize that she had automatically straightened her shoulders and thrown out her chin. The stranger, however, did. A slight smile touched his lips as he folded his long length into a chair.

Fiona, stiffly erect, fought to keep from looking at the man sitting so nonchalantly beside her. He stretched an elegant leg and lounged comfortably in his chair. It was as though he were the only genuine article in the room. And in a certain sense he was.

"Fiona," said Cousin Charles. "This is Robert, Earl of Dreyford."

Turning stiffly, Fiona nodded. "Milord." Try as she might she could not avoid the pull of those hard green eyes. Why did he look at her like that? A little shiver of hope surfaced within her. Could His Lordship be seeking a governess? Would Charles actually let her go to a new position?

"Good day, Miss Byrne." The earl's expression remained distantly polite. "Fiona, I believe, is your Christian name."

"Yes, milord."

"An Irish name. But I detect little brogue."

"I . . . My mother was Irish." Fiona felt the words being pulled out of her. "But I've never seen my homeplace." In spite of herself a wistful note crept into her voice.

"And why not?"

"My mother's father disowned her because she ran off with an Englishman." She repeated the old story in a monotone. "Papa was a commoner, and poor. He grew even poorer. Mama sickened. We went from lodging house to lodging house.

Until—" She swallowed quickly. "Until she died. I was ten then. Papa didn't want to go on. So he left me with Cousin Charles. And then Papa was gone too."

His expression did not change as he listened to her. To block out the painful memories, she considered this strange lord. His face could not be called handsome. His nose was too hawkish for that. But he was quite striking. And powerful. She could tell that just by looking at him.

"I see. And you have never contacted your maternal grandfather?"

Fiona's lips drew together firmly and her chin lifted. "I do not beg, milord. He knows naught of me. And if he did, he would not care."

A furrow appeared between His Lordship's black brows and Fiona wondered if she had somehow angered him. Habit made her drop her glance and so she missed the way His Lordship's dark eyes went to her cousin's face.

But it was not her words that caused the bunching of his bushy black brows. Thoughtfully, the earl considered his peculiar reactions to this young woman. The sight of her seemed to have addled his wits, causing him to consider possibilities that under other conditions would never have crossed his mind.

Take for example, the gleam in Hinckley's little black eyes as they rested on her. The earl was no stranger to that look, having encountered it in such diverse places as White's celebrated Bow Window and Harriette Wilson's equally celebrated house of ill repute.

Certainly, he had never found it particularly disturbing before. The nature of things decreed that many young women should be left defenseless, lambs for the shearing. But the thought of this particular young woman being shorn of her innocence made him want to deal the fat Hinckley a facer or, better yet, run a rapier through his abundant middle.

As the earl watched, Hinckley's greedy eyes went once more to his cousin, and the tip of his wet pink tongue slid out.

Dreyford leaped to his feet and almost planted the imagined facer then and there. He was prevented from this unseemly behavior only by the restraining habits of many years.

"Hinckley," he said tersely, "a word with you. Over here."

"Of course, of course."

Hinckley's beady eyes gleamed and the earl tightened the reins on his self-control. He would not give in to the Dreyford temper. But he was quite sure that in his entire lifetime he had never encountered a more pitiful excuse for a man than this fat toad who now beamed at him.

"I've changed my mind," whispered the earl, his frown darkening. "I'll take the chit. But we must marry as soon as possible."

"Yes, yes, milord. I thought you might. She has a certain beauty."

Hinckley extended a fat paw, perhaps to guide the earl back to his seat. But a slight stiffening in His Lordship's posture made the merchant content himself with a gesture.

They returned to their respective chairs and the earl, settling into his once more, cast another glance at the young woman who had just caused him to discard a hard-held tenet of some nineteen years. Her resemblance to Katie was not as pronounced as he had first thought. But that mattered little now.

It was not precisely clear to him why he should feel so strongly about this young woman. She was not, after all, Katie Howard. But for some extraordinary reason that had become immaterial. He felt that he had cheated the devil, who in this case bore an amazing resemblance to Charles Hinckley. And in spite of the fact that he had just given his consent to being shackled for life, he was immensely and inordinately pleased.

"My dear," said Cousin Charles, and Fiona raised her eyes. In spite of his soothing tone, she expected trouble.

"I know this will come as something of a shock to you. But it is certainly a pleasant one. The earl has asked for your hand."

For one wild moment the room tilted. Fiona clung to the arms of her chair and closed her eyes. What a cruel joke. She had no doubt Charles would find such a thing amusing; but somehow His Lordship did not seem the type to stoop so low.

She opened her eyes to find a dark face close to her own. His green eyes searched hers. "Are you all right, Miss Byrne? I fear your cousin was rather abrupt in his announcement."

Fiona fought to regain control of her tongue.

"I . . . Yes, thank you, milord. I'm afraid it was a little unexpected." She sought for truth in the eyes so close to her own. "Is it . . . I mean . . . You really have come to ask for my hand?"

"Really." The earl straightened and resumed his seat.

"I do not understand." Fiona forced her features into a mask of composure she was far from feeling.

His Lordship's tone became crisp. "I should think the matter is sufficiently clear. I wish to make you my wife, the Countess of Dreyford."

"The Countess of Dreyford?" Fiona repeated. She knew she sounded stupid. But this was all some kind of dream. Cousin Charles beamed paternally and the stranger surveyed her from hooded eyes.

"I presume you have no objections to becoming a countess," Dreyford observed.

"Of course not." Bewilderment sharpened Fiona's tone. A marriage that would remove her from Cousin Charles's purview. A respectable marriage. Nay, more than respectable. It hardly seemed possible.

"I trust you have no insurmountable aversion to my person," His Lordship continued, in the tone of one confident of his own worth.

"If I had, I should be considered a real peahead," she returned with a spark of humor.

"Then I fail to see what else can stand in the way of our speedy nuptials."

"But, milord," Fiona protested, "I have never laid eyes on you till today. And, as far as I know, you have not seen me. Why should you offer me marriage?"

Dreyford's eyes once again swept over her in that look of intimacy that brought the blood to her cheeks. "Though you're brown as a gypsy and your clothing is nothing less than abominable, you have a beautiful face. And that hair, properly dressed, will do much for you."

His eyes traveled the length of her body and again she felt herself brought to the blush. "As for the rest of you . . ." He shrugged nonchalantly. "Your endowments are quite adequate. In the hands of the proper dressmaker you should make a credible countess."

Fiona's doubts were not resolved. A man like this did not just make an offer for a woman such as she. But with those eyes regarding her sternly, she could not protest again.

"I'm sure that Fiona is overjoyed, milord," Charles interjected. "As she says, it has all been quite sudden."

Fiona's thoughts raced in mad confusion. Perhaps marriage to the earl would not be so bad. At least he inspired respect. Something that to her cousin's dying day he would never achieve. Anything would be better than. . . . Her mind rebelled at the thought.

His Lordship helped himself to a pinch of snuff from an elegantly enameled box, expertly flicking his wrist. Then he stretched his long, well-muscled legs and sighed. "May I suggest to you that my time is rather a valuable commodity. I should like your answer."

"It's yes, of course, milord," Charles said quickly, only to be silenced by a ferocious frown.

"Let the girl speak for herself," said Dreyford. "She has plenty of understanding." He turned his eyes on Fiona.

He was not Lonigan, she thought. But she could respect him. Surely that was a sound basis . . . Dear God, Lonigan! Was she still married to Lonigan? Had their union been legal or not? She moistened her lips. "I am greatly honored, milord. But surely you wish to know more about me. There are things . . ."

The sound of Cousin Charles clearing his throat was a direct warning. Much as she wanted it to move, Fiona's tongue cleaved to the roof of her mouth.

"His Lordship knows everything important," her cousin said.

The meaning of this was clear: Lonigan was not to be mentioned. Fiona shivered. Her pleading eyes sought those of the earl. "Please, milord, may I speak to you in private?"

His Lordship cut off her cousin's protest with a gesture of his hand. "Run along, Hinckley. I wish to be alone with my betrothed."

The expression on her cousin's face was not lost on Fiona. For his own reasons Charles wanted this match. If she bungled it, it would go badly for her.

The door closed with a sharp thud and Fiona was left alone with His Lordship. Nervously she got to her feet and, courteously, he did so too. For several moments he stood silent, watching her obvious agitation.

Finally he spoke. "I must admit to some perplexity." He spoke in formal tones, though the stern lips quivered slightly as though suppressing a smile. "I did not expect to find hesitation on your part." Stretching to his full height, he preened a little. "In London I have been for many seasons considered a prime article—'best heart, best hand, best leg,' as they say."

Fiona was torn between admiration for the man's confidence and irritation at his arrogance. "No doubt," she replied somewhat dryly. "But you must realize, milord, that this is my first glimpse of you. And I, when I used to think on marriage, wished to marry for love."

The earl's fine features twisted in a moue of distaste. Something within him roared rebellion at the thought that Hinckley might touch her, that she might be forced to submit to him. But it was pity, not love, that had prompted him to take this woman to wife. "I trust you have long put such nursery notions behind you," he continued. "Had I desired a flighty, romantic young woman, London is full of pretty faces with empty heads behind them. I wish my countess to have some measure of understanding."

She met his gaze. "I have been so long out of the nursery, milord, that it is no more than a vague and pleasant memory. And the life of a poor relation is not conducive to ideas of romance."

Something flickered in her eyes. He recognized pain. He should; he was no stranger to it.

But she went on. "Nevertheless, I do believe

that love exists. And I have not given up wanting to experience it."

He shook his head and advanced toward her. "Are you afraid of me, Fiona?" he asked, a trifle surprised to discover that he felt actual concern. "Don't be. I assure you, I shall make a passable husband." Perhaps even more than passable, he told himself, aware that for the first time since he had reached manhood he was considering the institution of marriage with something less than complete antipathy.

"I do not doubt that, milord." Clearly he was experienced in the ways of women. Clearly he had had his share of inamoratas. She would be foolish not to realize that. And foolish to let it bother her.

"Then perhaps you are afraid you will not make me a good wife." He had moved until scant inches separated them.

"I . . ." Fiona began, but she could say no more. Those eyes of his had grown suddenly bright and warm. She felt them reaching deep within her. His fingers closed around her arms, pulling her against his waistcoat.

"Never mind," he whispered, his mouth above her ear. "I know enough for two."

Here was another opportunity. She must tell him about Lonigan. Whatever Cousin Charles said, whatever escaping from him had made her consider doing, she was still Lonigan's wife. In the eyes of God, if not in the eyes of man. But her tongue refused to move. Her mind filled with the impressions of her heightened senses.

"Don't worry, my dear," said the earl, tilting back her chin so that her eyes were forced to meet his. "We shall deal together famously, I've no doubt. And now for a little pledge to seal our troth." And he bent his lips to hers.

His kiss was soft and surprisingly tender. Something began to happen to her and she pulled back, frightened by the rioting of her senses. The earl seemed not to notice.

"Now, my bride-to-be," he said, looking at her in a way she could not fathom, "I shall leave you to your preparations. Which, judging from the look of you, will not be very time-consuming. Pack only those possessions you treasure. A small trunk should do. Perhaps even a bandbox. I'll send round a gown and the rest of what you need for our nuptials. We'll procure a new wardrobe when we reach the city."

He moved toward the door. "Oh, yes, we will exchange our vows day after next. Immediately after Constance's ceremony. I expect she will want you in attendance. Then we shall be away to London."

His lips curled in amusement. "I must beg of you, Fiona, my dear, to close your mouth. It ill behooves a future countess to gape like that. Surely you have heard of a special license? Until our wedding day." And, bowing slightly, he departed.

As Dreyford strode toward his carriage, he smiled. Thank goodness he had prevailed. But why had the chit hesitated? He had never considered that, after he had come to the point of making an offer, the woman would balk at accepting it. His smile widened, became soft and tender, causing his groom to blink in surprise.

But the earl's thoughts were otherwise occupied. He must find a gown and acquire a special license. He would not rest entirely easy until Fiona Byrne was out of reach of her fat cousin.

• *Two* •

THE CLOSED CARRIAGE bearing the Dreyford crest moved through the countryside toward distant London. Spring rioted outside the window. But Fiona's mind was intent on the events of the past two days. One moment she was the despised poor relation in danger of being forced into an even worse position, the next she was the elegant Countess of Dreyford.

And elegant she was, she thought, looking down at her smart traveling dress of dove-gray sarcenet. The dress fit perfectly, accenting a figure that was more than passable, as her eyes had told her that very morning in Constance's cheval glass. The same gown had served as her wedding dress. For, as the earl had pointed out, since they were to take the London Road immediately after the ceremony it was foolish to go in for all the folderol usual to such occasions.

Fiona had not demurred at this. The thought of standing before God's altar in a special gown had seemed a compounding of her sin. Try as she might, she could not stop the little voice that insisted that she was still Lonigan's wife. That she belonged to him and none other.

Fiona sighed. Even now she could not suppress a small shiver when she considered the fate she had so recently escaped. Fortunately, her cousin's awe of the earl had kept him polite and at a distance. And now she would never again have to fear that mass of flesh.

Thinking of this, she felt a positive surge of gratitude toward the man at her side. Whatever his failings, and she had no doubt they were considerable, His Lordship had rescued her from a very unpleasant situation. Again she shivered.

"Are you cold?" he inquired, his eyes resting on her politely.

Fiona raised her eyes to his. "No, milord. I was just thinking of something unpleasant."

"Your cousin Charles, no doubt," the earl replied dryly.

Fiona looked at him in surprise. "How did you know?"

His Lordship crossed his long legs and flicked an imaginary speck of dust from a polished Hessian. "A simple matter," he answered with a small smile. "I myself can think of nothing more unpleasant. I cannot imagine that living under his fat thumb was an experience to be envied. Especially for a young woman like yourself."

Fiona glanced at him sharply, but he was busy considering his coat sleeve. Did he suspect what Charles had intended for her? If so, she owed him an even deeper debt of gratitude.

Since he continued to inspect his sleeve, she allowed herself a long look at his person. He had been quite correct in speaking of himself as a prime article. In his dark coat, a coat that seemed to fit entirely without wrinkles, he was a fine figure of a man.

She experienced again the surge of pride that had surprised her as she stood beside him in the rectory. There was no denying it: he was an exceptional man.

Of course she did not love him. He had none of Lonigan's happy-go-lucky spirits and verve for life. But he was a man of substance. He certainly would not vanish during the course of a day.

Fiona pushed this disloyal thought aside. Something terrible had happened to Lonigan. Otherwise he would have returned to her.

"I trust everything went to your satisfaction," His Lordship said, turning to face her.

"Yes, milord. Though I did wonder how you knew to have the gown fit so correctly."

The earl's hooded eyes regarded her levelly, a smile playing about his mouth. "You forget. I held you in my arms."

Color rushed to Fiona's cheeks. To judge a woman's size by the mere *feel* of her? Surely no man could have *that* much experience.

His Lordship chuckled. "Perhaps I should not disabuse you of your engaging habit of taking everything I say so literally," he drawled. "But, since we are shackled for life, I think it best to deal straightly. Actually, the size was got by sending for one of your old gowns." He sniffed disdainfully. "I trust you brought none of that garbage with you."

Fiona smiled. "Your trust is not misplaced," she

said. "I took great pleasure in leaving my cousin's house as empty-handed as I entered it. And it is you I must thank for that pleasure."

The earl shrugged his broad shoulders, putting the seams of his coat in some danger. "No thanks are due. Any man would have done the same. I could scarcely have my countess running around in clothing fit only for a scullery maid."

This was true, she knew. "Still, I must thank you. After all, I came to you quite empty-handed."

For a long moment his eyes surveyed hers and she had the strangest feeling he was seeking something in them. "Not precisely," he said slowly, his tone that of a man having reached a difficult decision.

Fiona's breath caught in her throat. Her fears had been justified. This was all too good to be true. "What do you mean?" she asked, fixing her eyes on his face.

Dreyford's sigh was real and quite heartfelt. It had been clear to him there in the library that the chit didn't know about her dowry. Perhaps he should have told her then.

But he had felt such a need to get the girl out of there, almost as though she *had* been Katie. "I mean exactly what I say. You did not precisely come to me with empty hands."

In the silence that followed she stared at him. "I knew there was something," she said finally, her voice flat. "Will you tell me what?"

He regarded her soberly. Why hadn't he kept his information to himself? "I suppose I shall have to. Though I assumed you would know about your own dowry."

"My dowry! But I don't . . ."

Dreyford sighed again. "Some consideration of the character of your cousin Charles might be in order here. Obviously he kept it secret from you."

Fiona frowned. "I do not understand. Papa had nothing."

"Your grandfather, whom you say knew nothing of your existence, followed your father's wanderings with intense interest. And on his deathbed he left you a substantial dowry."

She stared at the hands resting so calmly in her lap. "He left me . . ." She turned to face him. "What exactly did he leave me?"

"A piece of land in Ireland. Not outstandingly valuable in itself, but of interest to me since it adjoins my property there."

"So that is why you wanted me." Her voice had not risen, but he disliked the look in her eyes.

He nodded, careful to keep his own features calm. "I judged it time to take a wife and saw no harm in pursuing my best interests in the matter." He had no intention of ever revealing that a moment of sentimental weakness had sent him charging into the fray, rather like a knight in shining armor. Though upon reflection, the fat Charles made a better pig than a dragon.

Dreyford eyed the woman beside him. He supposed she had some right to fly up in the boughs. But the dowry had been useless to her without a husband. And considering the circumstances. . . .

The habit of long years in which Fiona had assiduously suppressed her temper deserted her in one short second. "Your interests!" she cried, in a voice that caused the earl to regard her with surprise. "What of *my* interests?"

He shrugged. "I cannot see that being the Countess of Dreyford is so disadvantageous, most especially considering your previous position."

"You tricked me!" she cried. "You and that abominable Charles!"

Dreyford's mouth tightened. "I must warn you, Fiona, that I find your coupling of my name with that of the abominable Charles most distasteful."

"As if I cared!" she retorted, aware that she was being unfair, aware that she should stop this tirade. "A gentleman would have told me," she continued. "Let me know everything before I made my choice."

"And how would you have chosen?" he asked in carefully polite tones.

"I would have gone back to my homeplace," she cried, her voice breaking into a sob. "And looked for a husband who could love me."

"A futile undertaking," replied the earl. "The Irish are notoriously poor husbands. Good lovers, yes. But husbands . . ." He shook his head. "I'm afraid not. Besides, love is only cause for pain. You're better off without it."

Fiona's anger helped her conquer a tendency to tears. "Just because you choose not to love doesn't mean others don't want to."

His Lordship considered this for some moments. Finally he shook his head. "I really had thought you a woman of understanding. I did, after all, take you out of the clutches of the loathsome Charles. Did I not?"

"Oh, yes, indeed!" Her former gratitude had turned to bitterness. She knew it was not really his fault, but he was there. And Charles was not. "For a price, of course. But what is that between gentlemen?"

The earl's brows lifted threateningly. "I hope you do not mean to legitimize that miserable mushroom by applying to him the term 'gentleman.' "

Fiona was past thinking rationally. All those years of servitude when she had had the means to be free! If only she had known. She and Lonigan. . . .

She turned to Dreyford. "How is it that my inheritance has survived to come into your hands? Charles is not the most honest of stewards."

"Your grandfather was a wise man," the earl replied. "He hedged your portion about with so many restrictions that none of your father's relations could touch it, not even if they should marry you."

"Nevertheless, I've no doubt Charles profited well from your match to me," she retorted. "He would not have allowed it otherwise."

The earl sighed still again. It was plain he was finding this matter wearisome. "I hope I shall not regret my decision to be honest with you. Under ordinary circumstances I would never deal with your cousin. But in this case no one else had what I wanted. I suppose he will trade on his connection to me. His sort does." He shrugged. "Life is such that circumstances sometimes force us into unpleasant situations."

His eyes bored into hers and she had the uncomfortable sensation that he considered their alliance a prime example of such a situation.

"If you had told me," she persisted, "we could have worked something out. I might have sold you the land."

His Lordship shook his dark head. "No. It was specifically stated that neither you nor your male relatives could dispose of it. A further precaution against Charles, no doubt. Only by marrying could you have access to it."

Her temper flared again. "You seem to have all the answers."

The earl took this statement at face value. "I believe I have been rather longer in the world than you," he observed. "And it appears to me that you have little cause to cavil. All in all, I should think congratulations are in order. Becoming my countess is not exactly negligible." He had a momentary thought of the numerous mothers who had dangled their daughters before him with that express purpose in mind.

Fiona cast him a fiery look. "Nor, I suppose, is acquiring my land in Ireland."

His Lordship raised a dark eyebrow. "Temper, temper, dear wife." His fingers reached out to catch a strand of auburn hair peeping out from beneath her bonnet. He was experiencing an intense urge to touch this fractious creature. "Your Irish blood is showing. Actually, though, the land is valuable to me. It was this that constrained me to deal with your reprehensible kinsman. In the hands of the wrong person that land could have been a thorn in my side. As it is, I can feel myself safe." He considered her blazing eyes. "In the matter of land, at least."

He captured her fingers, ignoring her protests as he did so, and peeled off her glove. The hand he examined was small, with slender tapered fingers and skin roughened by hard work. "Your hands will not suffer any longer, my dear," he said, dropping a sudden kiss into her cupped palm.

Fiona drew back her hand with a little gasp.

The earl's eyes darkened. It had not occurred to him that the chit might actually take a dislike to him. Women seldom did. And the other day, that tender little kiss of betrothal . . . "Such maidenly modesty ill behooves a married woman, my love. You must learn to be more wifely."

"Must I?" she snapped.

His Lordship's eyes flashed. The Dreyford temper was stirring. Already this business had tried his patience sorely. It was unconscionable that she should turn against him in this fashion. "Listen to me, Fiona. I am not regarded as a man particularly versed in patience. Though in your case I have worked mightily to cultivate the virtue. It might be a good idea for you to emulate my example. I have eyes and what is considered quite adequate understanding. I did not misread the gleam in your oversize cousin's glance, nor the evident relish with which he recounted your numerous charms."

Fiona felt the blood rush to her cheeks. He was right, of course. But why did that have to matter? Surely she was justified in her anger too. After all, she had been cruelly cheated.

When she did not reply, he smiled quizzically. "I cannot imagine that you are so lacking in understanding as to prefer that lumbering elephant to my more refined person."

She greeted this attempt at humor with a snort of contempt and was irrationally pleased to see lines of strain appear about His Lordship's hawkish nose.

"I see there is no question of dealing with you in such a mood," he replied, his even tones giving no indication of the irritation she knew he must be feeling. "So I shall leave you in peace to cultivate a better frame of mind in which to greet your wedding night." And with that he turned his attention to the landscape outside his window.

Fiona, too, turned her face to the window. Sold for a piece of land. And to a man of so little feeling that he counted her fortunate for the fact.

Dimly some part of her mind recalled to her that not so long ago *she* had been counting herself fortunate. But the little whisper of reason was drowned in the mad clamoring of outraged emotion.

She blinked carefully and swallowed a sigh. Weeping had long been a forbidden luxury. Certainly, she did not want to start now, even though it seemed that the unshed tears of all those long years were dammed up behind her eyes, waiting for the moment of release. She did not intend to let this man see her cry.

She must come to grips with herself, she thought crossly. Little as she might care for the prospect, she was now the Countess of Dreyford. And unless His Lordship should decide to ask Parliament for a divorce—a most unlikely possibility—she would remain so. Therefore she had best consider how to conduct herself.

If only she had not lost Lonigan. Those golden days gleamed in her memory, days of love and laughter. Some mishap must have overtaken him or Lonigan would have returned to her.

So she was doomed to this loveless marriage. To love, honor, and obey, she thought with bitterness. The very vows she had made to Lonigan.

With a barely audible sigh she leaned back against the velvet squabs. She was so tired. The strain of the last days had drained away much of her strength. And still before her lay a most difficult night.

Fiona struggled slowly up out of a haze of sleep. There was a decided stiffness in her back and one leg had fallen numb. Besides the cramping of her limbs, she was aware of a slight chill that had overtaken her right side. Her left, however, was cozily warm. For a moment she could not comprehend where she was. Then the warmth beneath her moved and memory came racing back. Clumsily, she jerked herself erect.

His Lordship's eyes glowed mysteriously in the

light of the carriage lamps. "No need to be flustered," he said in that dry tone she was beginning to find annoying. "There is nothing indecorous about a wife leaning upon her husband while she sleeps." His hooded eyes traveled over her, marking her evident consternation. But his expression gave no evidence as to what he was thinking or feeling.

Fiona busied herself with straightening her bonnet and gathering up her gloves. "Where are we?" she asked.

"We have reached London. And Grosvenor Square. We are home."

Home. She had never known a real home. Only the imaginary pictures she had painted of her homeplace. Besides, without Lonigan no place could really be home.

His Lordship eyed her critically and quite suddenly she felt wrinkled and dusty. He, by contrast, seemed as impeccably turned out as when he stood by her side before the altar. His hawkish nose twitched slightly and Fiona stiffened, but the earl merely patted her hand and said, "I am sorry for the discomfort of such a prolonged journey, but the press of business demands my attention tomorrow early. And I did suppose that you would wish to be present at Constance's nuptials. Otherwise we might have made a more leisurely return."

"I am quite well," Fiona replied, trying to match his noncommittal tone. "A trifle tired, perhaps. But a good night's sleep should mend that." She gave him a grave look. Apparently he was willing to forget their earlier disagreement. "I appreciate your concern for Constance. I was not to attend the wedding, you know. Before you came."

The earl's face took on an expression of distaste. "So I ascertained. How fortunate for England that all her cits do not manifest the miserliness of your cousin. I should fear for our survival as a nation."

Fiona managed a very small smile. "I shall add my thanks to yours. And I shall count it a great favor if we need never speak of my cousin again."

The earl's smile was grim. "That is one favor I shall grant gladly. *I* shall never introduce his name into conversation. And now, shall we go in? Berkins should be ready. I sent a rider to alert him some time ago."

Opening the door, he stepped out and turned to help her. For a moment Fiona stared at her husband's extended hand. Then, clutching her skirts with one hand, she placed the other in his grasp. His fingers were strong and warm, and, though she still felt some antagonism toward him, strangely comforting.

Though life was returning to her cramped limbs, she was yet a little unsteady, and when she reached the ground it continued to move beneath her feet. Her fingers grasped the earl's arm as she leaned against him for support. "A moment, please, milord. Until I find my legs again."

As she looked up at him, the glow of the link lights cast harsh shadows on his face. She felt uneasiness trembling in her breast and without thinking she pushed herself away from his supporting arm, setting off alone for the dark bulk of the house looming against the night sky. Suddenly he was beside her, scooping her up into his arms. "Milord, put me down! This is unseemly!"

The earl did not break stride. "No more so than having you go weaving up the walk like a drunken sailor. Besides," he added, ignoring Fiona's gasp of outrage, "this should appeal to your romantic soul."

There seemed little use in kicking like an angry child, though she definitely felt the urge to do so. His arms held her against him and he strode along quite easily. Fiona resigned herself to lying still, and tried to ignore the discomfiting idea that she could easily grow to like it, there against his chest.

The front door opened silently as they approached it, and Fiona glimpsed the butler's face. A man of much service, Berkins. Not a muscle twitched as he greeted the earl and calmly closed the door behind him. "The rooms are ready, milord."

"Very good, Berkins. The grooms will be bringing in the luggage. You needn't have it brought up till morning."

"Yes, milord."

From her position in His Lordship's arms Fiona could catch only snatches of the magnificence around her. But she saw enough to convince her that the house was truly an elegant one, a fit background for His Lordship.

Dreyford took the stairs easily and carried her

into a large room. Fiona sucked in her breath as he set her on her feet.

His Lordship stood, a supporting arm still around her waist, while her gaze swept the room. Her eyes lingered on the huge bed, its curtained depths mysteriously dark, before they moved to what was obviously the connecting door to his room. Fear and anger mingled in her breast.

The man beside her chuckled, a sardonic sound to her frightened ears. "If you are to succeed among the ton, my dear wife, you will have to cultivate a less transparent countenance. Your every thought is reflected there on for the world to see."

Fiona's knees trembled and she did not look up at him. "I . . ." she began, but no more words would come.

Strong hands turned her to face him and, loosening its strings, he tossed her bonnet lightly into a chair. "I fancy your hair," he said. "Candleglow makes it gleam like burnished copper."

Fiona summoned a little of her previous anger. "A monetary comparison quite in keeping with your character," she said crossly.

The earl chuckled. "This should prove a most interesting marriage. I am quite pleased." His eyes traveled intimately over her face and she forced herself not to back away. She would not let him see that she was frightened.

"I have acquired a woman of beauty—and spirit." He traced the curve of her lips with a warm finger. "Yes, I believe I shall enjoy our marriage."

Somewhat to his amazement, the earl realized that he was speaking the truth. He was actually pleased that in a moment of appalling sentimentality he had made this intractable young woman his wife, that he had bound himself for life to a woman he scarcely knew.

He watched her, guessing that she did not know how to answer him. "Silent, but not submissive, I trust." He could not resist teasing her. No more than he could resist folding her into an embrace.

Its effect on him was startling. Such embraces were hardly unknown to a man of his experience. But along with the familiar warmth of desire came a quite unexpected surge of tenderness.

The earl determined to examine it at some later date. For now he smoothed back the hair from her forehead and smiled down at her gently. "Good night, lady wife. Sleep well."

Fiona stood there as he crossed her room and disappeared through the connecting door to his own. It had been a short kiss. More tender than demanding. Nevertheless she was still conscious of the feel of his arms, the warmth of his body, the pressure of his lips. But, even more disturbing, came awareness of her body's response. Like a bird in a cage, it clamored for release, to soar upon the magic his lips promised.

This couldn't be, shouldn't be, she told herself numbly. This man was not Lonigan. Such special feelings should be reserved for the man she loved. Not given to a stranger, however legally he might consider them his due.

Then, hardly knowing what she did, she hurried across the room to turn the ponderous key that stood in the lock. And very softly, through the thickness of the heavy door, came the sound of His Lordship's cheerful whistling.

• *Three* •

THE CLOCK HAD struck eleven the next morning before Fiona awoke. In the dimness of the huge curtained bed she stretched her stiffened body and flushed as she recalled the events of the night before.

Fatigue had been too much for her and she'd removed the dove-gray dress and sought the softness of the big bed clad only in her chemise. She had hoped for the prompt comfort of sleep. But in spite of her exhaustion she tossed and turned for long hours. Waiting for the man who had not come.

A timid rap sounded on the door. "Yes?" she called out.

The door creaked slightly as it opened. "It's me, Yer Ladyship. The maid—Millie."

"Come in, Millie."

The girl advanced to the side of the big bed. "His Lordship says he's going to take you to Bond Street. So's you'd better up and breakfast. I need some time to make you ready."

Fiona was about to reply that she could get herself ready. But remembrance of her new station in life stopped her tongue. "Of course. Has His Lordship breakfasted yet?"

"La, Yer Ladyship. The master's always up and about at the crack of dawn. He ain't fashionable in that respect. Though you couldn't find a better turned-out man in the whole of the city. And the ladies, why they—"

Millie stopped suddenly and turned away. "I'll just open the curtains, Yer Ladyship. It's a rare golden day, it is. And then I'll be bringing up your breakfast. Will you be having chocolate and rolls? Or will you be wanting more? Sure, you could use a bit of fattening up."

Fiona smiled. "Chocolate and rolls will be sufficient this morning, Millie. I will eat heavier later in the day."

"Yes, milady." Millie's eyes surveyed the room. Was she looking for evidence of His Lordship? Fiona wondered.

"I'm afraid," she remarked calmly, "that I will have to wear the dove-gray on the chair there. You might see if it needs pressing. My baggage appears to have been lost."

"La, milady. To think of all yer pretty gowns lost." The maid's eyes grew wide. "But mayhap they'll turn up yet."

"I do not think so," Fiona replied, thinking of the drab brown gowns that she had cheerfully consigned to the flames before leaving Hinckley House. "I collect that is why His Lordship and I are to visit Bond Street. To replenish my wardrobe. And now, if I might have my chocolate."

"Of course, milady. Right away." Millie was

off immediately, her eyes gleaming in anticipation of new gowns to come into her charge.

Fiona lay back among the pillows and surveyed the room. It was a lovely place, done in shades of green. The hangings on the great bed were of forest green, as was the coverlet under her hands. The walls of the room, however, were so pale a shade as to be barely green at all.

The rug that covered the floor revealed an intricate Oriental pattern of greens, browns, and rusts. The chaise, artfully ranged by the fireplace, was covered in the palest shade of peach. And the delicate lyre-back chairs near the wall sported upholstery of muted green.

Yes, Fiona thought, it was a lovely room, the rich cherry of the wood furnishings in warm harmony with its colors. It was also, she realized belatedly, a fine setting for a woman of her coloring. But that must be coincidence. The earl could not have known ahead, could not have planned all this.

Yet beneath her fingers the coverlet seemed very new. And the hangings on the great bed did, too. He had not told her when and where he had first spoken to Charles about their marriage.

Well, if he'd designed this room as a foil for his new countess, he had certainly done a commendable job. In such surroundings, she could hold court with the greatest of them.

Fiona let her memory retreat to those long-ago days when Elvinia had painted for the awestruck young girls the word picture of a society lady's boudoir. How she received in her rooms while still dressing, though doubtless it was only the finishing touches that visitors were permitted to see.

It had been difficult for the child to understand why Elvinia found this so exciting, since the older woman was always careful to assure them that society ladies were raddled with disease, their cheeks pocked beneath the white powder and rouge, their figures falsely trussed and buttressed.

But eventually Fiona had discerned the truth: Elvinia's descriptions were colored by jealousy. For no matter how much wealth the avaricious Charles succeeded in amassing, the wife of a cit could never hope to be invited into the inner circle of the ton.

To the young Fiona, these grand visions had seemed unreal. Her happiest memories were of days spent in the ordinary rented rooms where she had lived with her parents. A new gown or a string of beads, though her acquaintance with them was minimal, were nothing to her. When she longed for something, it was the happiness of those lost days with her mother.

Fiona sighed. This new life, in spite of its apparent luxury, was not going to be easy. Her eyes moved of their own volition toward his door, where the key still stood in the lock. His cheerful whistling last night had unnerved her. She might have supposed him to insist on his marital rights.

But he hadn't. And this way he had of smiling at her, as if they shared some secret, was most unsettling. Orders she could comprehend. Shouting she was used to. But this behavior was a new experience.

A brisk rap sounded on the door. She barely had time to hear it before the door swung open to admit His Lordship. "So, I see you have wakened at last. I hope my lady wife is not going to be a lay-abed."

"No," she replied, trying to keep her tone even. "I am usually up and about at the crack of dawn."

His Lordship's mouth curled in amusement as he settled himself on the edge of the bed. "I don't believe that early rising is necessary," he said, his thigh brushing her hip through the coverlet. "In the city ladies seldom rise before noon."

Why hadn't he taken a chair? His nearness was very disquieting.

"How do you like your room?" he inquired, turning toward her.

She tried to collect her thoughts. "It is quite lovely." His eyes were warm. It was then she recalled that under the coverlet she wore only a chemise. She clutched the material with nervous fingers.

He smiled and reached out to touch her cheek with a gentle finger. "I thought it would suit you. I mean to do well by you, Fiona. No one has ever accused me of being clutch-fisted. You'll not regret our bargain."

She regarded the elegantly clad male shape of him. Evidently he had just come from business, but his morning coat was immaculate, his cravat blinding in its whiteness, and his well-polished boots reflected the sun. He'd been quite correct, if a little toplofty, in saying that he was a fine figure of a man.

But some perversity drove her to pick up the previous day's quarrel. "I regret it already, as you well know."

The earl's sigh was heavy. He'd hoped to find her in better temper this morning. Still, he could afford to be patient. They would be together for a long time. It struck him rather forcibly that this prospect did not bother him as it once would have.

But then, the marriage had cost him nothing. He was not going to live in her pocket. He would have others when he chose. And now, at least, London's mamas would keep their whey-faced daughters out of his path.

He had lost nothing—and he had gained much. A piece of Irish land he had long coveted. And a beautiful wife.

He would try another approach. "Fiona, my pet, there is no point in regretting what cannot be changed. Surely you must see that. Be logical."

Fiona swallowed. Her anger *was* foolish. She knew that Cousin Charles was probably right. Her marriage to Lonigan was most likely a sham, a trick to cheat an innocent girl of her chastity. Yet those golden days gleamed in her memory. And although it was illogical and ungrateful, she held His Lordship responsible for their loss.

"It's easy for you to speak of logic," she said stiffly. "You have everything you want. While my chance at happiness is gone." It was with difficulty that she kept back the tears.

She saw the lines of strain begin to etch themselves again along his nose. Then he captured one of her hands, disentangling it from the coverlet. He raised it to his mouth, his lips seeking her palm and lingering there.

"I must remind you, lady wife, that I do not yet have everything." His lips touched the tips of her fingers in a subtle caress. "But we shall soon remedy that deficiency."

"Milord . . ." she began. But he dropped her hand, and his mouth moved to cover hers. Surprise held her motionless for a long moment while his mouth explored hers, while her body wakened to a sweet delight. Then suddenly he sat erect.

To her consternation she realized that she had not heard, over the thudding of her heart, the rustle of skirts that heralded the maid's return.

"You may give Her Ladyship breakfast now, Millie," he said, as calmly as though he'd been caught reading a book. "We shall leave the house at one," he added cheerfully. "Until then, my dear."

And Fiona was left to choke down her breakfast under the admiring stare of the maid.

Precisely at one, Fiona descended the great stairs. The dove-gray dress had been pressed to perfection. And Millie, murmuring little sighs of appreciation, had helped her into it. It clung to her in a way that gave her some confidence. So did her hair, piled beneath the matching bonnet in a style that Millie asserted was the highest fashion.

Still, Fiona found herself fearful of meeting His Lordship's eyes.

He stepped out of the library and strode to the foot of the stairs, his eyes on her descending form. Fiona felt a shiver travel down her spine. This man was her husband—according to the law, her lord and master. And she knew him only in his most superficial aspects as a bored man-about-town trying to be patient with a woman he deemed foolish.

She had to admit that he might well be right in considering her foolish. But there was right on her side too. Marriage was the most intimate of institutions. And she would never have entered into it in this way if it hadn't been for the specter of Cousin Charles, his beady eyes gleaming.

But she had promised herself to forget Charles. He signified nothing now. The man before her was her future.

His Lordship's eyes rested critically on her face as she reached the bottom of the stairs and stood before him.

"You are still not recovered from our trip," he said. "I am sorry that we must go out today. But gowns take time to make, especially as many as I plan to order. And they can be stitched while you are resting. Then, when you are suitably outfitted, we shall burst upon society in a blaze of splendor."

Fiona laughed nervously. "If you please, milord, I believe I should find a subtle introduction more to my taste."

His Lordship smiled as he tucked her arm

through his and received his curly-brimmed beaver from Berkins's waiting hand. "I see that you have not looked in your glass this morning, my love. Otherwise you would see that a blaze of glory is the only way possible to us. How can you expect to ease yourself quietly into the ton when your hair and your figure demand everyone's attention? To say nothing of a heart-shaped face and eyes so warm they melt a man's soul."

A small sigh escaped from the lips of the maidservant Millie, who was plainly lost in admiration for the earl's style of compliment.

"You are so kind," Fiona replied sweetly as they swept out the front door toward the waiting barouche. "But then," she added for his ears alone, "a man such as yourself is practiced in the art of flattery. So practiced that he can make it seem even natural."

The earl raised a black eyebrow. "I hope that you are not about to take me to task for being a man. Indeed, having reached the age of three and thirty, it would seem rather odd had I no experience in these matters."

"While I, at three and twenty, am properly supposed to know nothing," she replied as she allowed him to help her into the carriage. It was folly to argue like this. She spoke to him as she would never have dared speak to Charles. But, somehow, she couldn't stop herself.

He settled onto the squabs beside her and gave her a strange glance. "Of course. Women know nothing of these matters. Good ones, at least. The others are different."

He smiled. "I should not think you would do well in that line. You haven't the disposition for it."

Fiona, thinking of how easily she might have become one of "them," did not rise to his bait. Even now, if he knew about Lonigan, he would be greatly angered, even outraged. But it would not be because he cared for her; it would be because she had come to him damaged goods. Because his property had been tampered with, because she belonged to him in a sense that could never be reciprocal.

Fiona sighed. The injustice of it was bitter.

His Lordship crossed his elegant legs, smoothly muscled beneath his wrinkle-free inexpressibles. "Well now, we shall have a busy time of it. First to the dressmaker. Madame Ormond has the reputation of being one of the city's finest modistes. When she dresses you, you are worthy of the first stare of fashion. Then we will frequent the bootmaker, the milliner, and sundry others whose job it is to furnish you with all those little luxuries of life that women of fashion find so necessary."

Fiona turned toward him. "Do you truly propose to launch me into society?"

His Lordship's black brows rose indignantly. "How could you think otherwise? I am not some miserly nipcheese who intends to relegate you to the country while I enjoy myself in the city. You will have all the amenities that traditionally accompany your position in life."

Fiona sighed. "Everything except love."

His Lordship's mouth tightened. Why did the

woman have to talk of that? He wanted to forget love, forget Katie. No, he would never forget her. Or the indescribable joy he'd felt just being with her. But the cost of that joy had been too high. He would not open himself to such pain again.

"I fail to understand why anyone needs love," he continued. "I know it is much touted in romantic novels. But I should think a sensible woman would prefer security. Love does not feed the belly. Nor clothe it. As more than one runaway has discovered to her chagrin. Yet women persist in this futile search for it. A search doomed always and inevitably to failure. Since even when love is found, it proves a fraud."

Fiona turned toward him. "You speak, milord, as one who has suffered love's pangs."

For the merest instant he was afraid he had given himself away. But she could not know. She was only guessing. "You mistake me, lady wife. Love and its pangs are equally unknown to me. And as a man who values the rational, I take great pride in the fact."

Fiona said no more on the subject. It was clear to her that he had loved and been hurt by it. But she did not contradict him. His Lordship was not a man one could contradict with impunity.

About that time the carriage rattled to a halt. The earl descended and turned to help her. Almost automatically now, she put her gloved hand in his and stepped down.

Madame Ormond's establishment was small and discreet, so discreet that the bronze plate bearing her name could not be read from more than four feet away.

Fiona felt a sudden rush of anxiety. Fortunately, Cousin Charles had had Constance educated as a lady. And since Fiona was forced to accompany her everywhere, she had picked up a great deal of knowledge concerning the ways of quality. But she had never in her wildest dreams imagined that such knowledge would be useful. And she was far from believing that she knew everything she would need to know.

"I know nothing of fashion," she whispered as she tucked her arm through his. "How shall I make choices?"

The earl's gloved hand covered hers in what could only be called a comforting pat. "Don't fret yourself, my dear. I did not imagine you would. I, however, am popularly accounted to have infallible taste."

Fiona could well believe this, but she did not see how it could help her. "But how am I to proceed?"

"You must look upon me with ardent eyes," replied His Lordship, his lip curling slightly. "Knowing us newly married, the modiste will think you besotted with me. As any number of women have been," he continued casually. "So, when you defer to my every whim, she will find there evidence of your feeling for me and not your lack of fashionable knowledge."

"I have come from the country, not the stage." She knew her voice was rising, but she could not control it.

The curl to His Lordship's lip was even more pronounced. "Imagine yourself the heroine in one of those reprehensible novels of drivel that women are always poring over. That should serve admirably."

There was no time for Fiona to fashion a suitable reply since by this time they had reached the door. The interior of Madame Ormond's establishment was dim after the sunlight in the street. Fiona blinked and clutched the earl's arm.

"Milord. Welcome."

A very tall, very slim woman approached them out of the gloom. Fiona could hardly believe her eyes. Madame Ormond had the figure of a stick, straight up and down, not a curve anywhere. She was clad in an expensively cut black gown that only emphasized her severe figure.

"I am honored to have you choose my establishment, milord."

The modiste's sharp gray eyes slid over the new client expertly, taking in every inch of her. Every flaw, Fiona thought with distaste.

But Madame Ormond knew her business. "Oh, yes, milord. You have done well. A jewel."

If the words had been gushed, Fiona would have discounted them. But delivered as they were in that cool, dispassionate voice they were quite effective. Fiona began to feel more warmth toward the dressmaker.

"We are here to get the jewel properly set." The earl smiled. "I judge that between us we shall make my lady's arrival into the ton an outstanding one."

The modiste nodded. "Indeed, milord. I'm sure we shall." She turned and preceded them down the hall. "Let us go to the private rooms. You know, of course, that her hair— But then, what might have been an obstacle for some will only contribute to our achievement."

Fiona, trailing along on His Lordship's arm, swallowed a sudden giggle. They were so serious about the whole thing. How could any one person's clothing be that important?

But she was soon to realize that no matter how she felt about the subject, both the earl and the modiste considered it of the utmost importance. They pored over pattern books, discussing the lay of a bodice or the puff of a sleeve with an intensity that astonished Fiona, whose acquaintance with fashion had been of the most limited kind.

She was particularly curious at this kind of behavior on her husband's part, especially considering that she had locked the door against him the night before. She had been angry with him then, and she was angry with him still, in spite of the looks of simulated adoration she managed for the dressmaker's benefit.

And here he was, devoting the whole of an afternoon to the purchase of her wardrobe. It was a sobering situation. She knew instinctively that Dreyford was not the man to spend hours with a modiste. But why was it so important to him that she be well dressed? There was his reputation, of course. He would not want to be labeled pinchpenny.

But there was more to it than that. Could he

possibly be trying to placate her? To appease her anger over the inheritance by this display of thoughtfulness? For thoughtfulness it was, that much she was forced to admit.

After her measurements were taken, the shop-girls brought bolt after bolt of material. Fiona found herself standing in the middle of the room while this fabric and that was held up to her face, considered against her hair, rejected or retained. Her ears rang with their names: jaconet, spotted cambric, muslin, striped silk, sarcenet, merino, satin, lamé, crape, net, velvet. Her eyes swam from the onslaught of so many colors. After years of drab browns and grays so much variety was overwhelming.

Madame Ormond regarded her with narrowed eyes. "The new color is yellow, as you know, milord. But with her hair— No, it simply will not do."

The earl's eyes also rested on Fiona speculatively. "No, I think not. I shall leave most of the patterning to you. Just remember what I have told you."

Madame inclined her head in acknowledgment.

"But I have in mind several gowns for the evening," Dreyford continued. "One of this green silk. Low on the shoulders. Décolletage to here."

The indication of his fingers across her bosom, though they did not actually touch her, caused Fiona to draw in her breath.

But the earl continued. "A bodice fitting to the waist. Her normal waist. None of that high-waisted foolishness. And a skirt that flows out from the waist. Without a train. Do as you please in decorating it. I can never remember the names for those gewgaws. But leave the bodice plain."

Madame frowned in concentration. "A little puffed sleeve, milord?"

"Very small. Nothing to detract from the purity of the line."

Madame nodded. "Yes, indeed. Very effective, milord."

"And the other, of a similar cut, though you may train the skirt. It should be of pale peach satin, trimmed in dark brown. You will know how to do it. The rest I leave to your discretion. Oh, and two morning robes in the same colors. I have a fancy for her in them. You choose the materials. I believe that's all for now. But perhaps you should read over the list."

Madame read. And Fiona, listening, lost track of how many gowns he had ordered. How could this be happening to her?

"One last thing," said the earl, rising to his feet and pulling Fiona to hers. "If it is at all possible, I should like to have the green silk by tomorrow, late in the day. Kemble is doing *Othello* tomorrow night. And I wish to take my new lady."

Madame Ormond's eyes narrowed as she calculated. "I have several girls I can put on the job. However, if I could hire two extra ones, I should be more certain of finishing in time."

"I shall pay the extra wages, of course," replied the earl as he led Fiona toward the doorway. "We'll expect the gown in the afternoon."

"Yes, milord. And the others will be done within the fortnight."

Then the earl ushered Fiona out through the shop and into the carriage which carried them to the bootmaker, the glovemaker, the milliner, and others.

By the time they had finished, Fiona felt wilted with fatigue. This shopping was more tiring than any task Cousin Charles had ever set her.

The bottom of the carriage was littered with boxes: gloves, bonnets, several Indian shawls, nightdresses, and even, to Fiona's acute embarrassment, a dozen new chemises. His Lordship's aplomb as he assisted her in the acquisition of these last items had been incomparable.

When finally he announced, "That's the last of it, now we can go home," she was exhausted. She was also inclined to look upon him with more friendliness.

The earl was not unaware of her change of feeling. The afternoon had been entertaining. And so had her company, especially as they had not had occasion to quarrel.

He also admitted to himself that he had enjoyed her simulated looks of adoration. Perhaps someday. . . .

He came close to chuckling when he realized that he was actually wishing for his wife to become besotted with him! What hilarity that piece of information would raise at White's. But of course it would never be known there.

What went on in her boudoir was private. And

tonight something *would* go on. He smiled at her warmly.

Wearily, Fiona returned the smile. Gratitude, though Cousin Charles had not done much to nourish it, was no stranger to her. It was clear to her that the earl's behavior had been exemplary. All in all, she was inclined to be kind to him. "I must thank you, milord, for your concern today. It was generous of you to accompany me. I should have had no idea how to proceed."

The earl smiled. "I was well aware of that fact. But no thanks are required. When you know me better, you will realize that I have sound reasons for everything I do. And kindness is seldom one of them."

His eyes grew suddenly veiled. "I have chosen a wife unknown to the ton. All eyes will be upon her. For my sake it is imperative that she appear a diamond of the first water. I have never appreciated being the butt of jokes. And I do not intend to begin by presenting a country bumpkin as my wife."

All this was said in his usual dry dispassionate tone, but Fiona felt her newfound kindness toward him rapidly vanishing. How absolutely arrogant the man could be!

The memory of those dispassionate words returned to her that evening when she retired to her room. His Lordship had informed her of an engagement, one made previous to their nuptials, he said. And one that he found it necessary to keep.

So Fiona stood alone in the lovely room she was

now convinced he had had decorated for her. She let Millie ready her for bed and then dismissed her. Several hours alone stretched ahead. She was not yet used to these long hours in which no demands were made on her. It was, in its own way, quite unsettling.

First, she opened all the wardrobe doors and chest drawers and examined her new purchases, marveling as a child might at such bounty. Then she sat down before her dressing table and began to brush out her hair.

The nightdress she wore, a wonder of softness and whiteness, was one of that day's purchases. But the silver-handled brush and comb set had been on the dressing table when she had first arrived. He had provided so much for her. Far more than was necessary.

She sighed. But he was not Lonigan. He was not the man she still regarded as her husband. She wanted someone to love her. And in spite of Cousin Charles's caustic remarks and Lonigan's failure to return, she had never been able to believe that her handsome Irishman, with his fair hair and laughing eyes, had left her of his own free will.

The two of them hadn't had much. His fortunes were at the ebb, Lonigan said. Soon, though, they would turn. Everything good would come their way. But for Fiona, everything good was already there. Having Lonigan she had no need of anything else.

With a sigh, she put down the brush and moved to the window. In the fading light she could just make out the courtyard garden where the flowers of spring were beginning to bloom. How strange to have a garden, to have a room that was her own.

How many weary times she'd dreamt of her homeplace. Though she'd never been there, she'd imagined fields lush with green grass, trees towering to the sky. A pleasant place where a child's tired body could lie in the grass and rest, where refreshment could be found for body and soul.

But she was a child no longer. And the earl had taken her land.

With a sigh, she crossed the room to turn the key in the door to the hall. Of course, some would say that she had not really lost the land, that what was the earl's was also hers.

But Fiona knew better. Everything she had—from the new nightdress on her body to the flesh it covered—belonged to His Lordship. What she had, she had purely on his sufferance.

She glanced toward the connecting door, and then, as though compelled by some force outside herself, she scurried across the room to lock it. Shivering, she blew out the candle and crept between the curtains into the great bed.

It was not unfamiliar, this feeling of being owned. But with Cousin Charles it had not taken quite the same direction. Certainly she was better off here. Yet there she had had a certain freedom of spirit. Every day *could* be the day Lonigan returned. Now even that would not matter, could not matter, because she belonged to another. Not even Lonigan, if he were by some miracle still alive, would dare to confront the Earl of Dreyford.

The closing of a nearby door made her sit bolt upright and clutch at the covers with trembling fingers. The earl had returned. And it was not late.

Trembling from head to toe, she slid silently down into the bed and pulled the covers up around her neck. Every footstep in the next room threatened to stop her breath.

She bit her bottom lip to stop its trembling. It must come eventually, this consummation she so dreaded. But tonight, with Lonigan so bright in her memory, she could not bear it.

She eased her breath out in a long soundless sigh. And it came—the sound her ears had been straining to hear. Her body went rigid as footsteps crossed his floor and a knock sounded on her door. "Fiona." His voice was muffled by the thickness of the door. But she could hear the urgency in it. "Fiona. Open this door."

Hardly daring to breathe, she kept silent. And finally, incredibly, his footsteps receded and utter silence reigned in the room.

• *Four* •

THE NEXT MORNING found a bewildered Fiona at the table in the breakfast room. His Lordship did not seem at all the type to take the thwarting of his wishes lightly. Cousin Charles would have long ago been purple in the face.

Now, regarding the ample meal placed before her, Fiona was puzzled. Somehow she had expected more from the earl than the jovial good morning with which he had greeted her. So eminently civil had he been, so beaming and cheerful, that the servants, too, were beaming. But Fiona had cause to suspect such false cheerfulness in a man so completely accustomed to having his own way.

It was not that she did not recognize his point of view. She was fully aware of it. It was only that last night the thought of him striding through that door and finding her in her nightdress had thrown her into a fit of the terrors.

It was for this reason that she had judged it expedient to rise and dress immediately upon awakening. She did not want to repeat the performance of the previous morning when His Lordship had found her yet abed.

But his hearty cheerfulness as he finished his meal and rose, reminding her of their theater engagement for the evening before striding off in boots so polished that direct sunlight on them produced a glare, was very unsettling. Perhaps it was because she knew he had no reason for such cheerfulness, indeed, had reason to feel quite otherwise, that she found her appetite small and the rest of the day most irritatingly long.

When it was time to dress for the theater, she was heartily pleased that for a while at least she would have something to occupy her mind other than His Lordship's strange behavior. Millie was in absolute raptures of delight over the new gown. Fiona had to admit to herself that she found it very attractive.

The cut His Lordship had commanded for the bodice, combined with the dropped waist of the gown, served to emphasize the swelling curve of her bosom. And although it left her neck and shoulders bare, it was not actually immodest. After all, she was now a married woman, long past the age of innocence and white muslin.

Its deep green silk brought out the hue of her hair, which Millie had pulled up high in the back, then allowed to cascade down in a riot of curls. "That there's the antique style," she said proudly, standing in rapt attention before the vision she had created. "La, milady, there won't be no more magnificent lady in the whole of Covent Garden."

Fiona, already flushed with pleasure over the reflection in her glass, allowed herself a small smile. "I do look rather well," she said. At least the sharp-tongued members of the ton could find nothing to criticize in her appearance.

"Rather well!" exclaimed Millie. "Why, if His Lordship wasn't already daft about you, he'd fall top over heels tonight. That's for sure."

Fiona accepted this compliment with a smile she felt looked as false as it felt. Then, taking a deep breath, she moved slowly out. Toward the stairs—and him.

Dreyford waited at the foot of the stairs. Would she ever get used to him watching her descend? Would she ever get used to *him*?

To occupy her mind, she made a mental inventory of his appearance. Coat of corbeau color, black silk Florentine breeches, black stockings and slippers. That he had a magnificent leg could hardly escape her notice. Nor, she supposed, would it escape that of the numerous ladies whose consciences were as easy as their virtue. His cravat glistened whitely in the light of the candles and all in all she could not find a single thing to fault him on. Except, of course, that he was not Lonigan.

As she came to a stop before him, the earl smiled. "I have chosen a veritable beauty," he said in a tone so warm that Millie sighed audibly.

"Thank you, milord."

Dreyford considered his wife. Why would her eyes not meet his? Was she thinking of last night and that locked door? He put down the sense of outrage that threatened him. Last night he had not given in to his rage and broken down the door that stood between him and the woman he wanted. The woman who was his. He was a man of breeding. There were other ways to attain his ends and he knew how to use them.

"I have some accessories to your gown," he said pleasantly. "They have been in the family for some years. It will please me greatly to have you wear them."

She looked up then, a hesitant smile on her lips.

He opened the box, showing her the heavy necklace of square-cut emeralds, the matching bracelet, and eardrops.

Her reaction was all he could wish. "Oh! They're beautiful!"

"Allow me to put them on you. I thought they would go well with this gown. In fact, I had them in mind when I ordered it."

Putting the box in Berkins's waiting hands, he extracted the necklace from its bed of black velvet and laid it around her neck.

He let his fingers linger there, on her nape, on the tender spot where tonight he would drop a little kiss.

She was so beautiful, far more attractive now than in that first moment he'd thought she was Katie. He was going to enjoy the married condition. And he would see that she did too.

Fiona's body quivered. There was something so intimate about the touch of his fingers. The heated blood rose to her cheeks. Fortunately, when he came around to clasp the bracelet, his attention was on her wrist and she had time to calm herself. Then he was smiling down at her. "I'm afraid I'm no hand at fastening eardrops. We'll let Millie do that for you."

Millie's nimble fingers moved swiftly and soon she stood back, an expression of gratified awe rounding her big gray eyes. "I ain't never seen such a beautiful lady," she declared stoutly. And then, clapping a hand over her mouth at her temerity, she gave His Lordship a terrified glance and scurried up the stairs.

The earl chuckled. "An excellent choice, that Millie," he told the butler, who was not quite successful in holding back his smile. "You may tell her that I am not displeased."

Berkins nodded. "Thank you, milord."

Then His Lordship tucked Fiona's arm through his and led her to the carriage. When he had settled her comfortably there, she turned to him. "What had Berkins to do with your choice of Millie as my maid?"

The earl shrugged. "The girl is the daughter of his widowed sister. The family is in hard straits. Millie had just lost her position through no fault of her own." He smiled. "I had thought to get you an older woman, an accomplished lady's maid. But I could find none without fault. To a woman they were all overbearing and rude. Not to me, of course. But to Berkins and the rest of the staff."

His eyes searched hers. "I shall replace her if she proves incompetent," he said softly. "But I thought you might be more comfortable with a young woman."

"I am," Fiona replied. "I enjoy her." She lowered her eyes. "Of course, she does flatter me."

His Lordship chuckled. "My, how quickly you have become a society lady."

"I?" Fiona's amazement was quite genuine. She did not think of herself as a lady at all. In fact, she had spent a good deal of that very long day wondering how she was going to react to the oglers who stared and the snobs who cut people dead.

His smile was warm. She could see that even in the dim light of the carriage lamps. "See?" he said. "You are already fishing for compliments. If you looked in your glass before you came down, you saw the same thing I saw. A very beautiful woman." His eyes gleamed and he tapped her cheek playfully. "False modesty is not a virtue, lady wife. You are a beautiful woman and you know it well."

For a long moment his eyes held hers, their green turning to glowing fires. A woman could sink, could lose herself in those eyes. Did he really find her beautiful? She felt something within her responding to him. When he looked at her like that . . . Suddenly his face was gone, obliterated by a picture of Lonigan's laughing one. And the moment was gone too.

The earl's eyes turned formal again. "Have you ever been to the theater?" he inquired politely.

Fiona shook her head. "Cousin Charles never brought us to the city. It would have cost him too much."

"Of course. I never saw a more miserly man." His eyes searched hers. "You are not sorry to have left his establishment?"

"No, milord, I am not sorry." Now, now he would mention the key, remind her of all she owed him, tell her not to lock him out again.

But he did not. Instead he turned the conversation to the evening ahead. "I am curious as to your reaction to Kemble's Othello."

"Does he do Iago also?"

The earl nodded, his eyes inquiring. "The story is familiar to you?"

"Yes, milord. Cousin Charles's library was large and impressive. He never read in it, of course. But after the last governess left, I spent many a rainy day reading to Constance. We found Shakespeare's work very interesting."

An increase of noise outside the closed carriage caused Fiona to lean toward the window. She drew back in alarm. "My word, Dreyford, the streets are thronged. What can be going on to make such a crowd?"

The earl's smile was amused. "It is nothing, my love. We are nearing Covent Garden. And it is the fashionable hour. The crush will be whispered about all tonnish London tomorrow."

He raised an eyebrow. "Ladies will report that it was too much for their delicate spirits. I trust that you are not given to the vapors."

Fiona shook her head. "I'm afraid Cousin Charles did not recognize such ailments. I don't believe Cousin Elvinia ever suffered from them either."

"No doubt she suffered enough from Charles and had no need of additional complaint," said His Lordship.

Fiona laughed. How good it was—to laugh at the man who short days ago had held life and death power over her. How very good.

The noise outside the carriage increased. Fascinated, Fiona watched the coachman maneuver through the crowd toward the place where others were dismounting. In so short a time that it seemed almost miraculous, the carriage had come to a halt and His Lordship was descending, turning to help her out.

She paused on the step. Behind him the pavement was full of ladies in brilliant jewels and beautiful gowns, of gentlemen in evening dress and uniform. They seemed completely oblivious of the din around them. Coachmen bellowed at horses and men alike. One of them spit out a string of epithets often used by Cousin Charles in fits of rage.

For a moment Fiona's face went white, the hand that rested in His Lordship's trembled.

Dreyford saw the spasm cross her features, felt the trembling of her hand. He saw her eyes widen in horror.

Automatically, he pulled her closer to him, a surge of unexpected tenderness filling his breast. Something had frightened her. "Fiona, what is it?"

"N-nothing. A memory."

So that was it. He had much to answer for—that fat pig of a cousin. And one day he would.

"Easy, my dear. Be easy. I am here."

It was perhaps a foolish thing to say, considering the circumstances of their union. But he *was* her protector. And she clung to his arm and flashed him a look of such gratitude that he felt immensely pleased.

He had done well in this marriage that had set everyone to talking. The poor relation had been transformed into a lovely woman. A very desirable woman.

A pert orange girl approached, flashing him a smile. But he shook his head. He wanted to get Fiona to the box, and chatting easily, he bore her along.

Fiona clung to the earl's arm. That momentary fear had passed. Charles could not harm her now. But this huge crowd was frightening. So many people—all so well and richly dressed, glittering with jewels, gleaming with gold.

And the theater itself, ablaze with candles and lamps, was richly gilded. With great effort she managed not to gawk about like a green girl fresh from the country. With even greater effort she ignored the prolonged stares of the oglers and allowed Dreyford to settle her in the box.

"There," he said. "You may relax."

This tender mood of his was disconcerting. Still, she strove for politeness. "Thank you, milord."

For some moments she occupied herself with looking around, trying to become convinced that this strange new world was truly hers.

She was contemplating a rather outrageous fashion plate in a pink waistcoat of the most horrendous hue and a cravat so tall his head seemed almost lost in it when the curtain went up.

The earl leaned forward. "Now," he said, "you are in for a treat."

Everything around her faded, forgotten as she was caught up in the drama.

So lost was she in the play that the intermission took her quite by surprise. She turned to the earl with a glowing face. "Oh, milord. I had no idea what a difference it makes *seeing* a play. The people are so very real."

"Indeed. I thought you might enjoy it."

"Oh, I do! It is absolutely marvelous." For the moment she forgot the greivance she had against this man. Like a child with a new toy she wanted to explore all its dimensions, to take it apart and see how it worked.

"Mr. Kemble is so majestic. Does he do comedy as well?"

Dreyford shook his head. "Sadly, no. The man's forte is the tragic." He made a moue of amusement. "He's a little too tragic for my taste."

Fiona frowned. "But, milord, surely the subject calls for that."

The earl shrugged. "Perhaps."

Fiona played absently with the fringe of her shawl. "And how should you have liked it played?"

The earl cast her an amused glance. "With a little more humanity. A man in such emotional pain doesn't necessarily declaim in rich round tones while striking heroic poses."

Fiona considered this. "Not being a man, milord, I cannot say. But what of yourself? How should you act in such a situation?"

For a moment Dreyford was silent. For a moment he thought of telling her. No one but Kitty knew of the tears he'd shed over Katie. And that was all behind him.

"I should not act in any way," he said. "Because I should not have loved as Othello did. To love is to give hostages to fortune. And that is not a wise move."

She nodded. "So Shakespeare says. But not to love leaves such an emptiness."

"My life is not empty," he replied. "There are other pleasures besides that of love."

She nodded. "Some lords play at cards for high stakes. Some race horses. And all keep—"

"Enough," he said. "Ladies do not speak of such." His smile was ironic. "Even when the Cyprians share the same theater with the wives, the latter do not recognize them."

She shivered. No doubt she was deploring his lack of feeling. But that wall he had built between himself and love had kept him going. That and the recognition that passion need have nothing to do with love.

"So you think Othello is foolish."

"Indeed, I do. Foolish on two counts. First, to chase that ephemeral nonentity called love. And second, to destroy his property."

He saw her shock.

"You needn't give me that look of outrage. Women have belonged to men from time immemorial. It is not something I designed."

"But you profit from it."

She looked as though she regretted that remark. As well she should. A woman in her position. . . .

The door to the box opened. "*Mon dieu,* Dreyford! What a beauty you have found. *Elle est magnifique!* Why did I not see you before?" Philippe de Noir raised Fiona's fingers to his lips in an exaggerated gesture.

"The countess has been staying with relatives in the country," said the earl. She was quick. She would catch his intent.

"Philippe and I have come to meet your new countess," said Roxanne. She leaned over to give him a kiss, the cut of her gown revealing her bosom almost fully to his eyes.

"Good evening, Roxanne." He turned to Fiona. "My dear, let me present Lady Roxanne Carstairs. And Philippe de Noir."

Dreyford swallowed a sigh. He'd always disliked Roxanne's pushy ways. The woman had no breeding. And she was not above revealing their former affiliation, which, for some unfathomable reason, he did not want brought to Fiona's attention.

Roxanne leaned closer. "I have missed you," she said, running a soft white hand across his lapel. "You have stayed away too long."

He couched his reply in polite tones, though he would have much preferred to give her a good shaking. "I have been occupied. The acquiring of a countess is not an everyday matter."

"I'm sure it is not." Roxanne's tone boded no good. Whatever had possessed him to ally himself, even momentarily, with such a harpy?

She was beautiful, of course. In a rather vulgar way. That display of bosom, for example, was in very poor taste. Fiona would never do it.

He looked toward his wife, but her expression had not changed. She was learning to present to the world the bored countenance that was affected by the ton. For a moment he wished to see her feelings writ plain across her face. He wished, he realized, to see jealousy.

He put a possessive hand on Fiona's arm. She turned and gave him a smile that dazzled his soul.

"Oh, Dreyford," she cooed, in a tone he felt calculated to put Roxanne in her place. "I am so happy."

And though he knew it would incense the other woman, he could not forebear responding, "Yes, my dear. As I am."

The other two could not take much of this billing and cooing and soon departed. As the door of the box closed behind them, the earl heaved a sigh of relief.

Hearing it, Fiona smiled. That outrageous woman had extended herself too far. She should never have touched him like that, in public. And imagine having the nerve to practically declare their alliance. Dreyford had been displeased. That excessive politeness of his was a sure sign of it.

The play began again and she dismissed Lady Roxanne from her mind. She had better things to think of.

When the curtain fell on the last act, unshed tears glimmered in Fiona's eyes. She felt the tragedy of such love. Perhaps because of her loss of

Lonigan. Of course, Cousin Charles's suspicions could be true. She was no longer the wide-eyed innocent whom Lonigan had talked into eloping to London and a marriage that could well be no marriage at all. But she still could not forget those wonderful days.

She turned to the earl. "Such tragic love," she murmured unthinking.

His Lordship shrugged. "Love is always a cheat," he said cynically. "And those who practice it are fools. On the other hand, jealousy is an emotion I find quite reasonable. It has to do with possession. What is mine is mine. No man may have it."

Fiona glared at him. Was he saying that he condoned Roxanne's behavior? How could the man be so unfeeling? "Let me understand this correctly," she said, anger creeping into her voice. "You do not believe in love."

"As I recall I mentioned that very fact. As I just said, love is only for fools." He raised a black brow. "And simple-minded young ladies whose brains have been addled by too much exposure to romantic novels."

At least he did not love Roxanne. She pushed the thought away. "You have never loved any living thing. Your mother, your father. Your horse, your dog." She saw the flicker of pain at her mention of his mother, but it was gone almost immediately.

"For my parents I felt respect," he said soberly. "For my horses and my dogs I feel affection. But I should be the first to admit that I do so, partly at least, because they are mine." He smiled briefly. "Just as for you, in spite of your rather provoking ways, I feel a certain affection."

"Because I belong to you."

"Of course." His serene expression betrayed no idea that he might be wrong.

"I should like to go home now," she said crisply. "I have the headache and do not care to see the afterpiece."

"A pity," replied His Lordship amiably. "It is rather an amusing one. But of course we must attend to your health."

His eyes told her clearly that he considered her behavior childish. But his tone held no reproach.

It was not until he had her settled in the carriage that he smiled and remarked, "An early bedtime will not harm either of us." Only then did she realize that she had hastened what she hoped most to delay.

The journey home was made in silence, the earl quietly regarding the city and Fiona planning how to elude him for another night.

But he made it all very easy. He left her at the foot of the great stairs with a smile and the words, "I believe I'll have a look at some papers before I come up."

She thought surely he would hear the beating of her heart, but he merely nodded to her quiet "Yes, milord," and turned toward the library.

Scarcely able to believe her good fortune, she sped down the hall and into her room, turning the key in the lock behind her. She was halfway to the other door when her mind registered what her eyes were telling her. The key was gone!

Frantically Fiona fell to her knees. Could the key have fallen? Could it be lying somewhere on the carpet? But the carpet was bare.

She tried to quiet her panic. There must be something she could do. She got to her feet. Maybe the door was still locked.

Her hand crept toward the knob. Slowly she turned it. It gave under her hand. Now she had no defense against him.

She looked around the room. The chaise! She pulled and tugged until she had wedged the chaise against the door. Then she dragged all the loose pieces of furniture she could move, piling them against it. Finally, panting, she retreated to the bed.

Millie's first knock went unheard. At the second, Fiona called out hastily. "I won't need you tonight. Good night, Millie."

In time she recalled she was still wearing her gown. Strangely, she had not injured it in her mad scramble to move things. With a glance at the door, she pried at the hooks and managed to loose them. Her fingers trembled so that she could not unfasten the heavy emerald necklace and bracelet, and she was forced to slip into her nightdress still wearing them. Cold and heavy, they hung about her flesh.

Like chains, she thought, creeping into the big bed and pulling the covers up over her trembling body. She knew she could not keep him out forever, but that was rational knowledge. It held no meaning for the trembling insistence within her that she could give herself to no man but Lonigan.

She tried to conjure up his likeness as she lay there in the flickering light of the single remaining candle, but her mind would not focus. Instead of Lonigan's fair face and laughing eyes, she saw only the dark earl, those green eyes of his alive with desire. Once she dozed off, and, imagining she felt his hands on her, was startled awake again. But the room was empty.

She took deep breaths, trying to calm her nerves. And then she heard the footsteps in the adjoining room. They approached the door. Holding her breath in the silence, Fiona heard the slight creak of the turning of the doorknob. Then there was nothing. She imagined His Lordship pushing his broad shoulder against the door, and her ears strained for the first sound of crashing chairs that would signify his success. Instead, she heard him breathing heavily. This was followed by the sound of muffled curses. The curses lasted only a few moments and then his footsteps receded.

She let out a long sighing breath. Safe for another night. Only another night, said a voice in her head. But in her relief she didn't care. At the moment it was all she could hope for.

• *Five* •

WHEN DAYLIGHT DAWNED, Fiona was already awake. The long hours of the night had passed far too slowly. And each succeeding minute had brought home to her the folly of her behavior.

Dreyford was certainly not accustomed to being treated in such a fashion. She could well believe that no woman had ever resisted him. And to have his own wife do so. . . . That must have been a blow to his pride.

She still could not fathom why such panic should have overtaken her. After all, she had been married before. She was not a schoolroom chit who trembled at the sight of a man.

Whatever its cause, however, this could not continue. Even a man of Dreyford's patience would not remain calm forever. Nor could she expect him to be. Any day, or more precisely, any night now, the famed Dreyford temper would evidence itself. And rightly so. At least to his mind.

She pushed back the coverlet and swung her legs over the edge of the great bed. It was a far cry from the trundle that had been her lot at Hinckley House. Just as this room quite surpassed any room she had ever expected would be hers. She ought to be grateful.

Slowly she washed and dressed in the new morning gown that had arrived with her evening dress. Madame Ormond's girls must have worked day and night.

Fiona sighed. She had much to be grateful for. From poor relation to countess was a grand leap. But it was hard to believe that this wasn't all a dream. That she wouldn't wake one morning and find herself back in Cousin Charles's power.

The thought made her shiver and she went to stand in the warming sunshine by the window that looked down into the little garden. Perhaps she could grow some flowers. That would be a pleasant way to pass the time that hung so heavily on her hands. She would ask Dreyford about it at breakfast—if she dared.

As it turned out, Dreyford was in fine spirits. He got to his feet, smiling at her genially as she appeared in the breakfast room door. "Come in, my dear. Come in."

"Good morning, milord." She hated the little break in her voice. But she couldn't help it. This genial mood of his was far more threatening than the screams and curses Charles had been wont to dispense. With Charles she had always known where she stood. But with the earl. . . .

Dreyford resumed his chair and turned back to his steak and kidney pie. A footman appeared to hold her chair for her. And Berkins bustled in to inquire what she would like for breakfast.

"Chocolate and rolls should suffice," she said.

The earl turned his gaze on her. His eyes gleamed with a certain merriment. "Come, come, lady wife. Best eat some real food. We've a busy day ahead of us."

"We have?"

He nodded. "Yes, indeed. Some more of your gowns should arrive this morning. And this afternoon we shall ride in Hyde Park."

"But . . ."

His Lordship smiled. "I've a fancy to show off my new lady. And my new team of high-steppers." He patted her hand, a gesture both unsettling and comforting. "You'll enjoy the park, my dear. Everyone will be there. I can point them all out to you."

Fiona sipped her chocolate, her mind in turmoil. "Milord?"

"Yes, Fiona?"

She had meant to apologize for the night before, to tell him she was ready to accept her wifely duties. But somehow her lips would not form the words. "What shall I wear?" she asked instead.

"Your gray traveling dress will do well enough. Did you sleep well enough, my dear? You're looking a little hagged."

Fiona flushed. When he used that tone the servants would think *he* was the cause of her tired appearance. But she kept her voice steady as she replied, "I slept quite well, thank you, milord."

"I'm pleased to hear it. A little fresh air will be good for you, however." He got to his feet. And before she quite knew what he was about he had dropped a quick kiss on her cheek and was gone.

* * *

The morning passed slowly. She filled it as best she could, walking in the little garden, reading from the books in the library, making a list of needlework supplies to order. But sometimes she found herself actually wishing for some duties. After all those years of dawn-to-dark labor this enforced idleness was hard to comprehend.

She wandered from room to room, trying to imagine what it would be like to be born to such splendor. But she could not. Her servitude was still too fresh in her mind.

She ate her lunch and contemplated the idea of always having enough to eat.

But first and foremost in her mind was the man who was her husband. Over and over she reviewed his actions. And always she concluded that he was not the sort to be kept from his rights.

She did not flatter herself that he felt any deep desire for her. Though sometimes his eyes seemed. . . . She pushed the thought away.

But she was sure of one thing. Dreyford was a hard man, a proud man. And what belonged to him belonged to him. In the fullest sense of the word.

Finally it was time to put on the gray sarcenet and wait.

The earl returned promptly. "Oh, milady," Millie said as she delivered the message that he waited below. "You look grand. No wonder his lordship's so took with you."

Fiona's smile felt strained. Perhaps the earl had missed his calling. He was putting on an admirable show. But she took the spencer Millie offered her and turned toward the stairs.

She should have waited for him in the library. Descending the great stairs under the scrutiny of those eyes was an unnerving experience. If only she knew what he was thinking.

Was his patience merely show? Or did he really not care? She almost missed a step at that thought. If he didn't care, perhaps he would never. . . .

The thought was oddly disappointing, but she had no time to consider. She had reached the bottom of the stairs. And the earl, wearing that charming smile that hid so much, offered her his arm. "So, my dear, we are off."

The park was crowded. Carriages and riders of all descriptions traveled around in a great circle. The crush was considerable.

"Milord, why does everyone come at the same hour? It's too crowded to do aught but walk."

Dreyford smiled. "So it is. I understand that in the mornings the park is quite empty."

"Then why don't we come then?"

The earl shook his head. "Fiona, Fiona. We don't come to the park to ride."

"We don't?"

"No. We come to the park to mingle, to be seen. Therefore we must all come together."

Fiona shook her head. What these people needed was some good hard labor.

"The ton has some odd tastes," the earl continued, "But we are no more odd than the common people."

Since Fiona had much acquaintance with the plight of the common people she was not prepared to hear them maligned. "How so, milord?"

"On Sundays everyone repairs to the park. Ladies' maids promenade in cast-off finery and fat cits parade their overfed daughters. The park is a veritable jumble of oddities then."

Fiona permitted herself a small smile. "Perhaps they are merely aping their betters."

The earl turned his eyes on her. "Aping, my dear?"

Fiona nodded. "Look at the lady over there—the one in the box coat and cape. See, she's wearing a round white beaver and a cravat." Fiona chuckled. "And Hessian boots. Surely this is not the peak of fashion."

Dreyford smiled. "Not now, perhaps. But it was once. That's the Countess of Ginsfield."

"Why is she dressed like that?"

"At the turn of the century there were some accomplished women drivers—female Jehus they were called. The countess was—still is—an excellent horsewoman."

"But that coat. It makes her look like a man."

The earl chuckled. "Perhaps. But underneath it the ladies wore fitted cambric gowns that concealed very little. In fact, some were rumored to damp their gowns."

Fiona frowned. "Whatever for?"

"To make them cling more closely to their limbs, of course." The earl smiled at her look of outrage. "Huggins," he called to the coachman. "See if you can bring us closer to the Countess of Ginsfield." He turned to Fiona. "I want you to meet her."

"A lady who damps her gown?"

The earl frowned. "That was youthful high spirits. For all her wildness, Kitty's a fine lady. Though perhaps she should give up driving now that she's past her prime."

Fiona's mind whirled. How oddly the ton conducted their lives. Damped dresses and ladies dressed like men.

Huggins maneuvered their carriage until they were beside the countess. "Kitty," called the earl. "Pull over there. I want you to meet my lady."

Fiona saw only a flash of smiling teeth and a red mouth before the lady pulled her team out of the path.

Huggins followed. The earl descended and helped her down. Then he tucked Fiona's arm through his and led her toward the countess.

"Kitty, this is my new lady, Fiona."

Bright blue eyes surveyed Fiona, then turned to Dreyford. "Robbie, you bad boy. How could you wed without telling me? And where did you find this pearl?"

"In the country, of course," replied the earl, his voice taking on a tone that Fiona had never heard before. She turned to look at him and could hardly believe her eyes. He seemed to have lost ten years. He looked almost boyish.

"Trust you to find a beauty." The countess laid

a gloved hand on Dreyford's sleeve. Instead of shrugging it off, he covered it with his own.

Seeing this, Fiona was surprised by a pang of jealousy. First Lady Roxanne, and now the countess. These ladies certainly took great liberties with other women's husbands.

"I never expected you to go off like this." The countess chuckled. "I thought marriage . . ."

"So did I, Kitty, so did I. Till I met Fiona. Then my fate was sealed."

The countess laughed, a warm rich sound. "So it appears."

As they chatted, Fiona searched the countess's face. Blue eyes, red lips, smooth cheeks framed by tendrils of dark brown hair that had escaped the beaver hat. If she were past her prime, she was hiding it well.

The countess linked an arm in Dreyford's. "Shall we walk?"

"Of course, Kitty." It was then Fiona knew. The knowledge came to her surely and without any great sense of shock. This was another one of his. . . . Dreyford and the countess had once been more than friends. Much more.

"So, Fiona has been living in the country," the countess continued.

Dreyford nodded.

"And who is helping her prepare for London life?"

"Why . . . no one."

Fiona, watching the earl's face, was astonished to see that the man was embarrassed.

"Dreyford, how can you expect the poor girl

to cope with our foibles?" The countess leaned around him. "Never fear, my dear Fiona. You will be well prepared. I shall do it myself."

"That's very kind of you, countess." Fiona heard herself actually accepting the help of this. . . .

"But, Kitty—"

"Nonsense, Robert. I insist." She winked at Fiona. "He thinks I may tell you all his boyish exploits."

"Kitty!"

Fiona was treated to the unbelievable sight of the Earl of Dreyford blushing like a schoolboy.

"Now, Robbie, there's no need for that. You weren't nearly so wild as Byron is."

"Byron?" Fiona asked, wanting somehow to spare the earl further embarrassment.

"Yes, he's all the rage now." The countess smiled. "Quite a dashing fellow in spite of his clubfoot. All those dark curls and that soulful expression. They impress women."

The earl snorted. "He should have gone upon the stage. He's so good at sighing and suffering."

The countess chuckled. " 'Childe Harold' is quite excellent poetry. Everyone says so."

"Perhaps," conceded the earl. "Speak of the devil," he continued. "There's George now."

"Yes. And Caro Lamb is still following him about." The countess sent Fiona a glance. "Caro's married, of course, but that doesn't stop her. She wants Byron. Silly thing, she believes love is all."

Fiona did not miss the sharp glance sent her way by the earl. She glanced again at the pair.

This poet was a strikingly handsome man. Dark and brooding. And the slender blond woman at his side engaged Fiona's sympathy.

Poor Caro Lamb. Had her family forced her into marriage? Made her the property of one man while she loved another?

The three of them made the circuit of the promenade and returned to their carriages. "I shall call upon you tomorrow," the countess said. "And commence your education." She climbed into her carriage and took the reins from her waiting groom. With a wave of her whip she was off.

"I hope she did not embarrass you," the earl said.

Fiona swallowed sudden laughter. It was far more likely that she had embarrassed the earl, but she did not say so. "Oh, no, milord. The countess is very entertaining. I'm sure she'll be a great help to me."

The earl's eyes had grown hard again. The boyishness had quite vanished. "Kitty's always been a wild one. I don't know . . ."

Quite to her surprise, Fiona realized that she did not want to lose the countess's friendship. Whatever she had once been to the earl, she was convinced that the countess was now willing to be her friend.

"Please, Dreyford. I am not offended by her frankness. Nor . . ." His face grew so grim the words almost died on her lips, but she forced a light tone. "Nor by her previous relation to you."

The Earl of Dreyford felt a distinct urge to voice some words unsuitable for female ears. He might have known Kitty would treat him like that. She always did. What he hadn't known—or even guessed—was that he would feel like that eager puppy he had once been.

He owed Kitty a lot, though. Too much to forbid her access to his wife. He didn't fear she'd divulge his secret. In all the long years since he'd spilled out his grief on her bosom, Kitty had not breathed a word of it. She would not do so now. And yet. . . .

"Please, milord. Say that the countess may call."

Fiona's hand still rested on his arm. Her eyes pleaded with him. "Please, milord."

"We shall see. But leave off talking about our previous relation in that tone. It's not proper." Actually, it had been the words themselves that set him off. Her tone had been quite unobjectionable.

Her eyes widened, those eyes so like Katie's. And the skin under her freckles paled, just as Katie's had. But her voice was firm. "I meant no harm, milord. Truly, I feel . . . that the countess wants to help me."

He felt it too. There wasn't a mean bone in Kitty's comely body. But it was damned inconvenient nevertheless.

"Very well," he said, unable to resist the plea of those eyes, and thinking himself about as foolish as man could get. "The countess may call."

Fiona's face lit up and she gave him a beautiful smile. The earl did not return it. Fool, he told himself. She did not smile because of him. She had locked him out of her bedroom. He, the Earl of Dreyford.

But she would smile at the prospect of friendship with a woman who had made quite clear her previous relation to him. Women, the earl thought sourly; could a man ever understand them?

He lapsed into silence. But soon they rounded a corner and came upon a group of screaming boys. Fiona leaned out the window. "What are they doing?" she asked. "Is someone hurt?"

The earl sighed. It was far more likely that they were tormenting one of their own. He leaned across her to look, inhaling a hint of perfume. She was so close. So desirable.

He could see nothing and the din increased. "Huggins," he called, "can you see?"

"Yes, milord. 'Tis a mongrel pup. Hurt, looks like."

"Oh, no!" Fiona cried. "They're stoning it!"

The earl sighed again. "Huggins, stop the coach." He took his time getting out. The crowd parted, making way, curious. A whimper came from the dog as another stone hit home.

He felt an unreasonable wave of rage. Why must the strong always batten on the weak? "Enough!" At the sound of his voice the urchins turned, a dirty, ragtag bunch, already hardened to any emotion but anger.

Sullen eyes stared at him from dirt-encrusted faces. He felt their animosity; it weighed on him like a physical thing. "Go!" he commanded. "Get out of here!"

For a second he thought the crowd would turn on him. But this was not France. Not yet. The boys slunk off muttering, and he turned his attention to their victim.

The cur snarled and bared its teeth. A spunky little thing, so filthy it was impossible to see its true colors. Well, at least the animal had a chance now. He turned away, but something made him take a last look back. And just as he did the animal gave a little sigh and sank to the ground.

Damnation! He could not go about London rescuing every stray. He muttered several other choice words under his breath. This penchant for rescuing the distressed was getting out of hand.

Nevertheless, he found himself moving toward the dog. It bared its teeth again, a feeble gesture of defiance. His nose wrinkled in disgust. The animal stank; there was no other word for it. And so would he once he touched it. No sense ruining a good pair of gloves. He shoved them under his waistcoat. With another muttered curse, he bent toward the animal. And drew back suddenly. It was with real surprise that he watched the blood well up along the thin red line where its teeth had grazed his skin. He chuckled. "That will do you no good," he said. "Fiona will tell you. When I rescue, I rescue."

He unwrapped his cravat and used it to immobilize the animal's jaws. Then, his lip curling in distaste, he lifted the creature into his arms.

Huggins's face was a study in amazement, but the earl hadn't the time to fully appreciate it.

"Open the door, Huggins. And quit gaping at me."

"Yes, milord. Right away, milord."

The earl deposited the animal on the floor of the carriage. More work for the stablemen, but they could use a dog. Maybe she'd turn out to be a good ratter.

Feeling naked without his cravat, he settled into the seat beside his wife. Only then did he look at her.

Tears stood in her eyes and one glistened half down her cheek. He felt an unfamiliar lump in his throat.

"You saved it," she said. "You picked it up yourself."

Only then did it occur to him that he might have let Huggins play knight errant and saved his clothes. He raised a deprecating hand.

"Oh, no! You've been hurt!"

He shrugged. "It's nothing. Some creatures always bite the hand that feeds them."

She winced, almost as though he'd struck her. Curse that wit of his! Now she thought he was talking about her.

He bent to stroke the matted fur and the dog's eyes lifted to his face. There was something in them, something he'd seen in Fiona's that first day. Fear, wonder, a desire to trust.

You've got bats in your attic, he told himself. *This is just a dog. And Fiona is just a woman.*

"She's afraid. We often lash out when we're afraid."

She accepted that with a nod. "Yes, I suppose we do. But why . . ."

He shrugged again. If he hadn't been so dirty he'd have put an arm around her. She wouldn't stop him now. "I felt like it. I wanted to." He chose his words carefully. "Now the dog is mine. No one will mistreat her. I take care of what is mine."

This was all very roundabout. But he wasn't about to tell her that the animal reminded him of her, that the streak of tenderness he'd thought buried with Katie was not only still within him, but making up for lost time.

Fiona gave him a sweet smile. "Whatever your reason, I thank you."

Her bottom lip quivered. He wanted badly to kiss it. And because he wanted to, he did—a small kiss, hardly more than a peck. She colored a little but said nothing.

"The dog will be all right."

Her eyes were still worried. "Are you sure? Those dreadful boys . . ."

"Yes, my dear, I am sure." He ran a hand over the dog. "She's bruised and dirty. Probably half-starved. But she'll survive."

He straightened and was surprised to see that the dog moved her bound head until it rested on his once polished boot.

The rest of the ride home was accomplished quietly. He moved the dog's head off his boot and climbed out. "Huggins, take this animal to the stable. Give her to Ben. You know, the boy who's so good with the horses. Tell him to wash and tend to her. Then bring her up to the house so we can see her."

Huggins nodded. "Yes, milord."

Fiona took the arm her husband offered her. The smell of the street was strong, but he had never looked better to her.

"I shall have to go bathe," he said, his nose wrinkling. "I smell like the gutters."

Fiona shook her head. "First we must attend to your hand."

"It's nothing, my valet . . ."

Fiona turned to the butler. "Berkins, we'll need soap and clean cloths. And some salt. We'll be in the library."

The earl straightened. "Really . . ."

"It's no use," she said. "I'm not letting you out of my sight till that scratch is cleaned." She saw the amusement in his eyes, but she didn't care. She couldn't tell him outright that she was sorry. That she knew *she'd* bitten the hand that fed her. But she could show her gratitude. At least as well as a dog.

"Milord?"

"Yes, Fiona?" He settled into a chair.

"What shall we call her?"

"Whatever you like."

She paused. "I should like you to name her. You saved her."

The earl smiled. Why had she never noticed the warmth in his smile?

"All right," he said. "Give me some time to think on it."

Berkins bustled in, followed by a footman carrying the supplies. He put them on a table beside the earl.

Fiona nodded. "That's all, Berkins. I can manage." She pulled up a stool. "Now, this may hurt."

The earl smiled. "I have been scratched before."

She felt the color flooding her cheeks. "Of course. You must forgive me. I am used to caring for Constance."

She took his hand in hers. It was a masculine hand, but the fingers were long and lean. Sensitive. She washed the wound carefully, pleased to see that it was shallow.

To his credit, he did not move a muscle when she sprinkled it with salt. He might have been sitting in anyone's drawing room, discussing the day's events.

She turned her attention to wrapping it. "Shall I survive?" he asked presently.

She returned his smile. "Yes, milord, I think I can guarantee that."

She left him at the door to his chamber and went on to her own. How complicated the man was. She had thought him cold, with no deep feelings. But a cold man would not dirty his clothes, or even his hands, over a stray dog. A cold man would have driven away and left the animal to its fate.

Fiona untied her bonnet and turned to put it on the table. And then she saw. The table was gone! The chaise was gone! Every stick of furniture except the four-poster and the huge wardrobe was gone from her room.

Complicated? The earl was Machiavelli himself. A bubble of laughter rose in her throat. There would be no barricading the door this night.

• *Six* •

By the time she descended the great stairs, Fiona was no longer quite so amused. She was beginning to like Dreyford, to see depths of humanity in him despite the dry, bored exterior he presented to the world. But no matter how she respected the earl, no matter how she admired him, she still felt married to Lonigan.

If only she had told Dreyford the truth that day. But then there would have been no marriage and Cousin Charles would have. . . . She put the thought behind her. There had been the marriage. She was safe now.

"Milord is in the library," Berkins said. "With the dog."

There was no intonation in Berkins's voice. Yet she knew quite clearly that he was pleased. And—she sought for a word—proud. Berkins was proud of his master.

So was she. "Thank you, Berkins."

Her soft evening slippers made no sound on the floor. In the library door, she stood, watching the tall dark man and the dog whose hair, now recognizably red and white, shone in the firelight.

"You're safe now," Dreyford was saying. "I'll

take care of you. I always take care of what's mine. Except, I couldn't help . . ."

Sensing her, he looked up and straightened. "Come in, my dear. If it weren't for her eyes, I'd never recognize her."

Fiona crossed the room to his side. "Ben deserves congratulations."

The earl nodded. "He shall have them."

"Have you given her a name?"

He shook his head. "Nothing seems quite right."

"Well," she said, settling on the divan beside him, "she's a very lucky dog."

He smiled and patted her hand. "Then I shall call her Lady Lucky. And I shall give her to you."

The dog's tail thumped happily.

Fiona chuckled. "I think not, milord. This dog belongs to you. And she knows it."

His smile was so warm. No wonder he had charmed so many ladies.

"But what is mine is also yours."

Perhaps, she thought, not really believing it, but unwilling to disturb their newfound accord by disputing with him.

The evening passed slowly. The dinner was excellent, but she found her appetite somewhat diminished. Tonight she would not be able to keep him out.

"You are strangely quiet this evening," he remarked as he led her to the library.

"I am—just thinking."

They chatted about this and that, about members of the ton, about which of Shakespeare's plays each preferred.

And then the earl said, "It's been a long day. I suggest we retire."

At the foot of the great stairs she hung back. "Milord, the dog. We have made no provision—"

The earl turned to face her. His eyes burned into hers. "Fiona," he said quietly. "Stop this. There will be no more tricks. Tonight is the night."

She wanted to accept this. She knew she had to.

"Berkins," the earl called.

The butler appeared.

"The dog will sleep in my dressing room. Put her there."

"Very well, milord." Berkins took the dog by the collar and led her away.

The earl watched until they were out of sight. Then, as though she weighed no more than a feather, he swept her up in his arms and ascended the great stairs. His arms were strong, warm. Her cheek rested against his silk waistcoat. Under it his heart beat, rapidly.

He pushed open the door to her room and deposited her between the curtains onto the bed, beside the nightdress Millie had laid out for her.

"I would retire to my chamber to disrobe," he said, crossing the room to close the door to the corridor. "But there seems to be some problem with the doors getting stuck."

Her heart had come up in her throat and was jumping about there, making it impossible to speak. It hadn't been like this with Lonigan. She hadn't been frightened then.

"So," the earl continued, "I'm afraid I shall have to risk offending your maidenly modesty."

He took off his coat, his waistcoat, his cravat. She wanted to turn away. This was all wrong. She was Lonigan's wife.

He took off his shirt and stood before her in his breeches. His chest was dark. A narrowing line of black hair went. . . .

"Perhaps you'd like help with your gown."

"No, no. I'll do it."

She turned her back on him. There would be no avoiding him this night. He was going to have what was his. Using the bed curtain as a kind of screen, she struggled out of her gown and into her nightdress. She was trembling as she crept between the sheets. And when she raised her eyes again, he was standing there, totally naked.

"Why?" she cried then, driven by her fear and some other inexplicable emotion. "Why must you have *me?* Hasn't London lightskirts enough? Isn't the Lady Roxanne willing?"

He frowned, raising a black eyebrow. "The Lady Roxanne is nothing to you. Or to me. We will not discuss her."

He pulled back the sheet and climbed in beside her. "I come to you because you are my wife. This is proper and right."

I'm not your wife. She wanted to scream the truth at him. *I'm Lonigan's wife. And I always will be.* But the words stuck in her throat. And anyway, his mouth was covering hers.

* * *

Later, when he was finished, he kept her beside him. It was rather comforting there, against his warmth. She felt something cold and hard inside her beginning to melt.

"Now you are truly mine," he said, wrapping a curl around his finger.

Her golden feeling started to fade. "Possession of my body is no guarantee you possess my heart," she retorted.

He laughed. "Perhaps not, my dear. But your body is here. Beside mine. Soft and warm. And quite beautiful."

He stroked her bare shoulder and she resisted the urge to burrow against him.

"I can see your body. I can feel it. But your heart . . ." He shrugged. "I shall settle for what I can see. Can touch."

The cold something inside her splintered, and cut into her, driving her to say, "But you shall never have my love."

He shrugged. "Why should I want it? People don't expect a man's wife to love him. The fashionable world being what it is."

Anger flared up inside her. It was so unfair. And so confusing.

A moment ago, in his arms, she had felt safe. Almost as though she'd found her homeplace. She rolled away, turning her back on him. "So. People don't expect a man's wife to love him. Then perhaps they expect her to love someone else."

His hand closed around her wrist and he jerked

her back into his arms with a force that drove the breath from her body. "There'll be none of that," he said, his voice gruff. "What's mine is mine—alone."

She didn't stop to examine the strange feeling of relief this sentiment brought her, but hurried on, determined for some reason she couldn't quite discern to taunt him.

"And what will you do?" she mocked. "Will you put me on bread and water? Lock me up in the country? Or abuse me as you just have?"

The body against her own stiffened, but he did not release her.

"Abuse?" Dreyford repeated. "Abuse?" The chit was going beyond the bounds. "Really, my dear, you'll have to do something about this penchant for the dramatic."

"I told you I was tired."

Her voice was low, muffled against his chest.

"You have been 'tired' for several nights now. And, as I told you, I am not a patient man."

"And so you abuse me."

It almost sounded as if she were laughing. But that could not be possible. This was not a laughing matter.

"You should not have denied me my conjugal rights."

Absently, he stroked her shoulder. "I am reputed an excellent lover," he said. "You may ask . . ." He stopped, aware of the absurdity of what he was about to say. Sometimes she drove him to the most peculiar actions. "That is, you have no cause to complain."

Indeed, she had not. He'd taken as much care with her as if she'd really been Katie. He'd used everything Kitty had taught him and all he'd learned since.

Fiona had responded to him, too. Not at first, perhaps. But later. And hers was not the staged passion of Harriette Wilson's crowd or the violent, almost devouring coupling that Roxanne craved. It was real—and still tinged with her innocence.

He kissed his wife's ear, and then her throat. All this talk was making him. . . .

Fiona tried to sort out her tumbled feelings. For a while there, in his arms, she had forgotten Lonigan. The earl must be the excellent lover he held himself to be: indeed, he had been able to reach her through her fear.

No man but Lonigan had ever touched her. She had expected a distasteful, abhorrent experience. And instead. . . .

His lips were raising those strange feelings again. He could melt all the coldness inside her. But it was only temporary. Some sort of delusion. Because she was still Lonigan's wife. And she should not be enjoying the caresses of another man.

She twisted her head to avoid his kiss and forced a brittle laugh. "Really, milord. It's not necessary for you to prove your point again. Surely one possession should suffice."

He did not show his anger, but she felt the change in his body. And although he held her just as close, she felt a chasm opening between them.

"Very well," he said, dropping a kiss on her forehead. "I shall respect your wishes."

The moment his body left hers she felt a sense of loss. A chill passed over her.

He got to his feet and stood there, naked, but with perfect aplomb. "Sleep well, lady wife. I shall."

And then he was gone, leaving his clothes on the floor for Millie to pick up in the morning.

With a sigh Fiona sank back into a strangely empty bed. "Dear Lord," she murmured, "what shall I do?"

And on the other side of the connecting door the earl pulled his nightshirt over his head and climbed into his own bed. The sheets had been warmed, of course. And besides, it was spring. But the bed felt cold nevertheless.

He sighed. It would have been nice to sleep beside her, to feel her warmth next to him all night.

And then he laughed. How the mighty had fallen! How many times had a woman begged him to stay the night? And always he had refused. But this was different. This was his wife, his Fiona.

He stretched and smiled. It had been a good beginning. Her attitude toward him had been changing for the better. Slowly, though, until today and the affair with the dog. He smiled. What would have marked him outlandish with his own kind had made Fiona like him more.

A sigh not his own startled him and he turned to find a pair of eyes looking at him with adoration. He reached out to pet the dog's head.

"If only *she* would look at me like that," he

murmured. "All right, Lady. You may sleep beside the bed. I guess I owe you that much."

The dog settled onto the rug with a small sound of contentment and the earl returned to his thoughts. Yes, rescuing the dog had put him considerably higher in Fiona's estimation.

He shook his head. What a pretty pass he'd come to. The Earl of Dreyford, the best catch of many a Season, not only leg-shackled, but acting like a foolish witling to boot. And not even caring.

Fiona woke late the next morning. She stretched and smiled a little. Last night had not been so unpleasant. In fact, the worst part had been trying to sleep after he left her.

Lying there, under the green coverlet, she tried to discover why she had done that, why she had driven him away when she really wanted him there. She sighed and rolled over—and met the dog's eyes.

"Lady, what are you doing in here?"

Warmth flooded her body. He must have let the dog into her room, let her in while she was sleeping. Had he stood looking at her? Had he bent to kiss. . . .

She threw back the covers. Enough of such foolishness.

She rubbed the dog's ear. "He must have gone out," she said. "If he were still in the house, you'd be with him."

The dog's tail thumped the floor.

Fiona sighed. Life was so much simpler for

Lady. Dreyford rescued her and she gave him her complete loyalty.

For a moment Fiona wished she could have done that, wished there had been no Lonigan. How could she wish such a thing? For years the memory of Lonigan had been her sole source of comfort, the only good thing in a miserable life. And now she was ready to forget him. And all because another man had treated her civilly. That was like forgetting her homeplace.

"No," she said aloud. "I won't forget him. I won't."

Later that afternoon Fiona sighed and glared at the needlepoint chair cover she was stitching. Ordinarily she was quite good at needlework. And she enjoyed it. But this day she couldn't seem to concentrate.

The dog was company for her. But she was also a constant reminder of the earl and what he had done for her.

Fiona had just stabbed her finger for the third time when Berkins announced, "The Countess of Ginsfield, milady."

"Oh, do send her in."

The countess stopped in the doorway. And Fiona stared.

Kitty was wearing a gown of white muslin, of the simplest cut, the sort a girl might wear before her come-out. Only the countess's gown was almost sheer, and it certainly didn't give her a look of innocence.

It was tied high, under her white bosom, with

a long black ribbon that streamed to the floor. And it left her shoulders, and her arms, and considerable bosom, bare. She wore no other adornment. She needed none.

Fiona got to her feet. "Lady Ginsfield, please come in."

Kitty took a chair and crossed her long legs, revealing black Hessians.

Noting Fiona's glance, she laughed. "Rather a silly getup, isn't it? But Ginsfield likes it." She smiled. "It reminds him of our salad days. Which are quite too far behind us."

She grinned. "And to be truthful, *I* like it. I don't mean to grow old till I absolutely have to."

Lady thrust her head into the countess's lap. "Well, what's this? I don't remember you."

Fiona finally found her tongue. "Her name's Lady—Lady Lucky. Dreyford rescued her from some awful boys."

Now it was Kitty's turn to stare. "He rescued her?"

"Yes. It was quite wonderful. He went for her himself. Picked her up and all. She snapped at him, nipped his hand. But she adores him now."

Fiona paused. "I'm sorry, Lady Ginsfield. I shouldn't run on so. I've very glad to see you. Thank you so much for coming."

"No thanks are necessary," Kitty said. "I wanted to come. And for mercy's sake drop that Lady Ginsfield stuff. Just call me Kitty."

"Yes, Kitty."

"Now, tell me. How did you and Robbie really meet?"

"I— Oh, Kitty, I'd like to tell you. But I don't know."

Kitty raised a hand. "Stop right there. If Robbie wants me to know, he'll tell me." Her eyes surveyed Fiona's face. "You know about us," she said.

Fiona considered lying. But she wanted to be friends with Kitty. And friends shouldn't lie. "Yes," she said. "I guessed."

"And you didn't take him to task? For introducing you to me?"

Fiona shook her head. "Why should I? I did not know him then. And I could see— There is affection between you."

Kitty smiled. "I believe I was his first." She scrutinized Fiona's face. "My dear, I don't mean to shock you. But Dreyford has had many women. You'd do well to accept that."

She smiled. "When he came to me, he was practically a stripling. But so proud. You must never get in the way of his pride."

Fiona nodded. She waited, wanting Kitty to tell her more, wanting to see Dreyford through someone else's eyes.

"We have not—been close like that for many years. But you're right, I have an affection for him. And he for me, I believe."

"You say he has had many women."

Kitty nodded. "Of course. But he will not thank me for telling you so. Strange, isn't it? Men do as they please and no one says a word. But if a woman—"

She paused. "I don't know how you think on

this, but a word of caution. Don't try to play Dreyford tit for tat. He may have his dashers. And the ladies will flock around him. But don't you try anything. He wouldn't stand for it."

Fiona swallowed despite the lump in her throat. The last thing she wanted was to complicate her life with another man. But she couldn't tell Kitty that.

"I shall not be interested in other men," she managed to say.

"And quite rightly so. Considering that you've got the best of London's Corinthians." Kitty leaned closer. "I tell you, my dear. No one ever expected Robbie to go off. It was a tremendous shock to hear the news. Robbie—leg-shackled. It's still hard to believe."

Berkins appeared in the door. "Another caller, milady. Lady Roxanne." He frowned. "I tried to suggest that you were busy, but the lady . . ."

Fiona took a deep breath. "Show the lady in."

Kitty nodded. "A wise move." She settled back in her chair. "I think I'll just sit her out."

Fiona had only time to smile her thanks before the Lady Roxanne appeared. Her walking dress of violet silk was tight to the point of vulgarity, but Fiona had to admit that it displayed her abundant charms.

"Good day, Lady Roxanne. How kind of you to call."

"I was passing. And I thought, I must stop to see Dreyford's lady. She will be alone and lonesome."

Fiona suppressed a smile. "As you can see, I already have a caller. But do sit down."

Roxanne nodded to Kitty, who returned the nod. Watching them, Fiona noted that though Roxanne was probably fifteen years younger, her face looked harder, older than Kitty's. Obviously, there was no love lost between the two. If Kitty didn't like Roxanne, perhaps Dreyford. . . .

Lady got up and went to investigate this newcomer. Roxanne gave her a little kick. "Dreadful animal, get away from me."

Lady snarled and retreated to Fiona's feet.

"Really," Roxanne exclaimed. "How can you keep such a vicious creature?"

Kitty's smile was enigmatic. "People have been known to keep all sorts of strange creatures," she said pleasantly. "And most of us snarl at those who try to harm us."

Roxanne shrugged. "I did not come here for a lecture. But to talk to Fiona." She glanced from Kitty to the door. "Don't let me keep you."

Kitty shook her head. "I just arrived. And I've come for a nice long chat."

Roxanne didn't greet this news with much pleasure. "Well," she said. "Since you're here, tell me the latest gossip. What juicy *on dits* have you been hearing?"

Kitty leaned back in her chair and, crossing her booted legs, idly played with the ribbons on her gown. "I've been rather busy. Ginsfield just bought a new pair of grays."

Roxanne shrugged. "Surely you don't spend all your time in the stables."

Apparently, Fiona thought, politeness got short shrift in the world of the elegant. She searched her mind for something to talk about. "We saw the poet Byron yesterday," she ventured. "He was walking in Hyde Park."

Roxanne's eyes gleamed. "Was Caro Lamb after him?"

"I—I believe they were conversing." Fiona felt a twinge of guilt. Caro Lamb deserved sympathy, not gossip.

"That woman has no sense." Roxanne tapped a foot clad in a heelless slipper the exact shade of her gown. "She's chased that man all over London."

Fiona sighed. "Perhaps she loves him."

"Loves?" Roxanne's tone made the word a joke. "Why would any sane woman commit such foolishness?" She licked her lips. Like a cat after eating cream. "I can understand wanting him. I mean, that dark melancholy look is very attractive. And those curls. But love . . ." She made a face. "Love is for puling babies. Give me desire any day."

Kitty wrinkled her nose. "You seem to have been given more than enough."

The air between the two almost crackled with animosity. Fiona, watching them intently, thought it almost like a play. It was fascinating to see what they would do next.

Roxanne shot a glance at her rival. "Certain people have had no complaints."

"Certain people," Kitty returned evenly, "are

sometimes carried away by their own desire. Or give in to ennui."

Roxanne bristled. "Dreyford was never bored. Oh!" She turned to Fiona. "Oh, my dear, I am sorry. I didn't mean to . . ."

Fiona knew the lady had done exactly what she meant to do. She smiled. "My dear Roxanne. Don't give it another thought. Robert has told me all about you."

Kitty's eyes held amusement, but Roxanne looked stunned. "He couldn't have. Dreyford never talks about—"

"Ah," said Fiona pleasantly, "but this is different. You see, I am his wife. You were only . . ." She dropped her eyes, but not before she caught Kitty's wide grin.

There was silence for several moments. Then Roxanne collected herself. "Well, I must be getting on. I've a lot of stops to make. So nice talking to you."

"So nice," Fiona echoed, wondering if such obvious lies were overlooked in heaven.

"Good day," said Kitty, a hint of merriment in her voice. "And good hunting."

Roxanne did not deign to reply to that.

They were quiet until they heard the front door close behind her. Then they both broke into peals of laughter.

"Are you sure," Kitty asked when she could speak again, "that you have been in the country? I have never witnessed a better set-down. You took the wind right out of her sails. But Robbie didn't tell you about her. Or about me. He's not that sort."

Fiona smiled. "You're right. I met Lady Roxanne during intermission at the theater. She made their affiliation rather obvious. Dreyford was not pleased."

"I should think not. I could never understand him taking up with that dreadful creature. She has no heart."

"Perhaps that's the reason." Fiona sighed. "Dreyford does not believe in love, you know. He has no capacity for it."

Kitty stared at her. "Poppycock. The man's capable of deep and abiding love."

Fiona wished that were true. But Dreyford had said it himself. He found love a cheat, a foolishness. There was little hope of him changing his mind.

"Be careful," Kitty said. "Roxanne may not believe in love, but she's no stranger to revenge. She'll want to get back at you. And she'll do it through your husband. You must keep him away from her."

"But how?"

Kitty chuckled. "Even in the country they must tell you how to keep a husband happy."

Fiona felt the blood rising to her cheeks. To actually invite him into her bed. . . .

Kitty's eyes were still on her. "Understand this about Roxanne. She was Robbie's latest. And she meant to be his last. Then you came along."

"But she doesn't love him."

Kitty shook her head. "Fiona, my dear, love has

nothing to do with marriage. As she said, Roxanne desired him. She also desired the position he could give her. And she's not going to be charitable toward the woman who usurped it."

Fiona nodded. "I shall do what I can." But she knew quite well that she could do very little. If Dreyford desired Roxanne, he would go to her. It was entirely up to him.

She was back at her needlepoint, sipping tea and considering the things Kitty had told her, when Dreyford returned. She heard his voice as he spoke to Berkins and stabbed herself with the needle again. The dog heard it, too, and hurried out.

By the time he reached thc library door, the dog at his heels, she had regained some measure of composure.

"Good evening," he said.

"Good evening, milord. Did you have a pleasant day?"

He selected a chair across from hers and settled into it, stretching his long legs. "It was tolerable." He smiled. "And made more so by memories of last night."

His look brought a blush to her cheek. And a pounding to her heart.

"And your day?" he inquired, absently stroking the dog's head.

"I had two visitors."

"So, Kitty did come."

"Yes. And Lady Roxanne."

Dreyford felt a wave of irritation. Why had he

ever become entangled with that creature? He composed his voice. "And what did the ladies have to say?"

"Kitty's visit was very pleasant. She was wearing one of those dresses you told me about—the kind they used to damp. I've never seen a gown so sheer. And Hessians."

He straightened. "Kitty can carry it off. Even at her age. I'm glad you like her. She'll be a good friend."

He shook his head. "But Roxanne is another story. What did she want?"

"First she told me her philosophy about love."

She smiled at him, but her eyes were troubled. If Roxanne had hurt her. . . .

"Her philosophy sounds very much like yours."

She was watching him, waiting for his reply. "How so?"

"She said desire's the thing. That love doesn't count. Don't you think that agrees with you?"

He didn't like the way this conversation was going. "What else did she say?"

"Oh, she did let slip that you had never been bored with her."

"Never . . ."

Her eyes were so clear, so ingenuous.

"You know, when she was your— During your previous relations."

He swallowed an oath. Roxanne had no right to flaunt herself before his wife. "And then what?"

The smile she gave him was genuine. He'd swear to it.

"Oh, she apologized for having revealed so much. But I knew she meant to. So I told her it was all right."

"You *what?*" He felt a pang of quite irrational annoyance. All right, indeed!

"Oh, I didn't encourage her to think she could continue. I just told her I knew about it. That you had told me."

"I? I never told a woman—"

"Yes, so Kitty informed me later. Actually, I had guessed. At the theater. The way she touched you. The way she talked to you."

She stopped to take a sip of tea, those eyes of hers so innocent over the Wedgwood rim.

"Kitty said it was the best set-down she'd witnessed in a long time."

"No doubt," he said dryly. But it would take more than wit to best Roxanne. "Take care," he said. "Roxanne is a vicious enemy."

"Yes, milord. Kitty said the same."

She laid her needlepoint aside and looked him directly in the eye. "Kitty asked me how you and I met."

"And what did you tell her?"

"Nothing, really. But I should like to. If you've no objections."

He shrugged. Kitty seemed destined to become the repository of all his secrets. "You may tell Kitty anything. She has never betrayed a friend."

"Thank you."

Fiona's eyes met his again. Like the dog's they showed gratitude. Perhaps even affection. He smiled to himself. Affection would be nice.

• *Seven* •

THE NEXT MORNING Fiona woke early. The earl had accompanied her to bed and when the morning light came peeping through the windows he was still there, sleeping soundly, with his arm flung across her body.

But the weight of his arm did not bother her. Actually, though she would not have told him so, she found it rather comforting.

He stirred and pulled her closer. His lips touched her ear, lingered there. "Good morning, lady wife."

"Good morning," she murmured.

From the floor came the sound of the dog's thumping tail.

The earl laughed. It was a sound she had never before heard him make—a sound of pure joy that made her heart want to sing.

He kissed her throat. "I'm sorry I can't linger here with you this morning, but I've matters of business to attend to. Shall we go to the theater tonight? You will have an opportunity to compare Kean's Othello to Kemble's. And I've a fancy to see you in that green silk again. Though actually—" His lips moved across her throat and down her shoulder.

With a sigh he threw back the covers and got to his feet. "But I must go. Lie abed awhile, my love. It's too early for a lady to be up and about."

"Yes, milord." She watched him step around his clothes, the dog instantly at his heels.

At the connecting door, he raised a hand in a farewell salute. "Till tonight," he said.

When Fiona woke again, it was to the feel of a wet tongue licking at her fingers. She laughed. "Lady! Whatever are you doing?"

The dog whined and her tail thumped the floor.

"All right, all right. I'm getting up."

Minutes later Fiona went downstairs, the dog at her heels. Berkins cleared his throat. "Ah, there you are, milady." He hesitated.

Something in his look alerted her. "Yes, Berkins. What is it?"

"I— It's the stableboy, milady."

"Ben?"

Berkins nodded. "The boy insists on speaking to you. I told him it was impossible." He frowned. "Stableboys do not make calls upon ladies. I'll send him back to—"

She shook her head, remembering the days when she'd been alone, with no one to turn to. "No, don't. Ben may always come to me. Send him to the library. I'll wait for him there."

The butler looked almost relieved. "Yes, milady. Right away."

Fiona took a seat in front of the fire, the dog

settling with a sigh at her feet. What could the boy want?

Ben came in, clutching his cap, his eyes round with wonder at the sights of the master's mansion. She saw him look at Lady and for a second the tension in his face eased.

She spoke to him gently. "What is it, Ben? Why do you wish to see me?"

"I—I—" He twisted his cap in work-roughened hands. "I needs yer help, milady." His lower lip quivered and he bit down on it.

"Tell me, Ben. What's wrong?"

"They's alaughing at me," he stammered. "All but Huggins. But I don't care 'bout the laughing. It's the babies I cares about." His eyes filled with tears and he swiped at them with the back of a grimy hand.

"What babies?" Fiona asked. Was the boy's family in trouble?

Ben swallowed. "They's agonna drown 'em. But Huggins said they hadda wait."

"Drown them? Ben, whatever are you talking about?"

"The pups," the boy sobbed. "They can't drown 'em. They's just babies."

Puppies! Fiona heaved a sigh of relief. "Come here, Ben."

He sniffed and edged closer, a hand going out to touch the dog that had come to his side. "I jest wanted to be like 'im. Like His Lordship. He saved yer Lady Lucky here. I wants to save these pups."

Fiona's eyes filled with tears. Ben was a good

boy. He deserved her help. "Where are the puppies?" she asked.

"Out in the stable." He sniffed again. "Huggins made the others wait. They laughed. They said you wouldn't help."

Fiona got to her feet and took his grubby fingers in hers. "Come along, Ben. Show me these pups."

The men stood respectfully and touched their caps when she came into the stable. Huggins coughed apologetically. "Ben's only a lad, milady. And he's tender of heart. Don't be too hard on him, please."

Fiona raised a hand. "There's no need to apologize, Huggins. You were right to send the boy to me."

The coachman allowed himself the beginning of a smile and she knew that he was on Ben's side. About the others she couldn't tell. They looked everywhere but at her.

"Where are the puppies?" she asked.

Ben led her to a nest of straw in the corner of a stall. "Here, milady. Ain't they something, though?"

Fiona nodded, suddenly unable to speak. The world was such a hard place for the likes of Ben; surely a little kindness could not go amiss. Let the boy keep the puppies.

The wriggling black and brown mass separated into individual pups. Their eyes were not yet open but they scrambled unerringly for their mother—and breakfast.

Ben looked up at her, his eyes full of pleading. "You ain't gonna let 'em—"

"No, Ben. The puppies will be safe."

She turned back to the others. "These puppies are not to be destroyed. Those are my orders." There was no sound from the men and no expressions on their faces. Except for Huggins. His smile broadened.

Ben's eyes shone. "Oh, thank you, milady." He drew himself up proudly. "I'll take care of 'em. They won't be no trouble."

An hour later Fiona was admitted to Kitty's drawing room. Kitty looked up from the fringe she was knotting. "Fiona! I didn't expect you today. Come in."

Fiona took a chair, but she found it difficult to sit still. "I—I have an idea. And I want to know what you think of it."

Kitty put the fringe aside. "Tell me, my dear. You look so serious."

Fiona edged forward. "That's because this is serious business. You know how Dreyford rescued Lady."

Kitty nodded.

"Well, this morning the stableboy . . ." Fiona launched into the story of Ben's puppies. "And so," she concluded, "I got this idea. To open a kind of shelter. A place for homeless strays. Do you think it will work?"

Kitty's usually cheerful face grew sober. "My goodness, I never would have thought of such a thing. I just don't know. But my dear, you're talking about a great deal of work. You must find a place for it. And have people to run it. And people to work there." She clapped a hand to her forehead. "Thinking about it quite makes me dizzy."

Fiona leaned forward even further. "But you do think it's a good idea? And you will help me? Really, Kitty, it will not be that much work. And think how much good you'll be doing."

"Stop!" Kitty cried in exaggerated alarm. "When you look at me like that, I would promise the most outlandish things." She grinned. "But why am I worried? Robbie will never let you do it."

"But if he consents, you will help me?"

That evening Dreyford helped his wife to her seat in Drury Lane. Amid the splendidly gowned and bejeweled ladies that filled the boxes, Fiona was the most beautiful of all. "So," he said, "tonight you get to see the great Kean in action."

Her smile gave him a warm glow. What an addlepated witling he was turning into. Countless women had smiled at him. And none of them had ever made him feel as she did.

The change in him had been nothing short of amazing. He had practically come to live in her pocket. Though he forced himself to attend his usual haunts, he was always eager to get home. To see the dog's tail wagging a greeting. And, even more, to see the light of welcome shining in his wife's eyes.

No one at White's could possibly have imagined such an end for him. He himself had always thought—

"Milord," inquired Fiona, her hand warm on his sleeve. "Is that Lord Byron? Down there in the pit?"

He looked. "Yes, my dear."

"But is he so impoverished? That is, why does a lord sit down there? Why doesn't he rent a box?"

Her innocence was so refreshing. So like Katie's. Strange, the memory of Katie no longer carried its heavy weight of pain. He could think of her almost with pleasure. "Of course Byron can afford better," he said. "But he likes it in the pit. Says he can see and hear more."

She nodded. "Who's that nice-looking young man he's talking to?"

He was instantly alert. "Don't tell me—" If Caro was at it again. . . . He searched the youth's features, then relaxed. "No, it isn't."

"Isn't who?" Fiona asked.

"It's nothing, my love. I thought it might be Caro Lamb."

She frowned at him. "Why should you mistake a young man for Caro Lamb?"

This was not a topic he wanted to pursue. He would have to learn to think before he spoke.

She gave him a small smile. "Come, husband, you can tell me. After all, I'm a married woman."

He chuckled and patted her hand. He was fairly caught. And she was right. He might as well tell her. She would soon hear about it anyway. "Of course, my dear. Well, Caro used to masquerade as a youth. She dressed as a page and followed Byron about the city. I thought perhaps she was up to her old tricks again. But that is not her down there. Perhaps William has got her in hand. Finally."

His wife's beautiful forehead wrinkled into a frown. "She cannot help it if she loves Lord Byron. If she was forced to marry against her wishes—"

"Forced?" He stared at her. She was carrying this love thing too far. "My dear, no one forces Caro Lamb to do anything. She wanted to marry William. And she did. Then she wanted to bed Byron—"

"Please, Robert—"

"Don't look so shocked. You are the one who wanted to discuss such matters."

Fiona felt herself blushing again. He always seemed to be in the right. "Yes, well, let us talk about the play instead. Or rather, about Mr. Kean."

Her husband smiled. She liked his smile. Lately it had changed, had seemed softer and gentler. Sometimes it even seemed to reach his eyes. And perhaps he was right about Caro Lamb. Perhaps.

"I would not interfere with your judgment of Kean," he said. "Though I fear that inadvertently I have already—"

The curtain went up. And there stood the celebrated actor.

"But he's so little!" The shocked exclamation escaped her unawares, and caused startled glances from several nearby boxes.

"I'm sorry," she whispered, mortified. "But he took me by surprise."

The earl smiled and leaned toward her. His warm breath caressed her ear and the memory of his kisses sent a frisson of delight skittering down her spine.

"It's all right, my dear. Everyone *knows* he's little. But you'll soon forget that."

She did not see how such a thing could be forgotten. But since she'd already committed one faux pas, she kept her tongue between her teeth and turned her attention to the stage.

And she discovered that Dreyford was right. When Kean spoke, his size became immaterial. Right before her eyes the man grew to heroic stature.

She sat fascinated, afraid to breathe for fear she would miss some special intonation, afraid to blink for fear she would lose some important piece of business. He was marvelous, he was—

When intermission came, she expelled a great breath.

"So." Dreyford touched her arm. "What is your estimate of Kean's performance?"

"He's magnificent, milord. Such power. His voice is like—like a musical instrument. And with it he plays upon our senses. And his eyes— So penetrating!"

The earl smiled. "And in contrast to Kemble?"

"The two are as different as night and day."

"And you prefer?"

"Kean, of course." She smiled at him. He was a good husband, one of the best. Maybe this was the time to ask him. But she hesitated. Perhaps it would be better to wait. Her idea needed some explaining. Better broach it later, after they had returned home and—

She felt the blood rushing to her cheeks. Surely there was nothing wrong with a wife telling her husband things in their bed. It was a logical place to talk, an uninterrupted place.

She turned her gaze to the pit where the dandies were on parade. One in particular caught her attention: a tall lanky fellow whose sky-blue uniform was almost covered with gold braid. She watched him bend to talk to someone. And suddenly the blood stood still in her veins.

It couldn't be. It couldn't possibly be. But that man, the one the dandy had stopped to talk to—that man looked like Lonigan.

And then he got to his feet and went out the aisle. She watched till he was out of sight.

When the play resumed, she was still staring after him. It was all a mistake, she told herself. A trick of the light. She'd been thinking about Lonigan so much that she imagined she saw him. She would just forget the whole thing, put it from her mind.

"Fiona. Fiona!" The earl repeated her name as though he'd already said it several times. "What is it? What's wrong?"

"I—" To her surprise she saw that the play was over. "I am all right, milord. I was just— The play was so intense. The emotions so strong. I was still—thinking."

He nodded. "Do you wish to stay for the afterpiece?"

"I think not." Seeing that man who looked so like Lonigan had been rather a shock. And her enjoyment of Kean's performance had suffered for it. But she did not intend to let such wild imaginings spoil her plans for the rest ofthe evening. Her idea was important. She must make Dreyford understand what it meant to her.

Later, at home, they lay in peaceful silence, their arms around each other. Fiona savored the loveliness of it. To feel so cherished was special. The earl ran his fingers through the hair at her neck. "You have lovely hair. I shall buy you a diamond tiara to wear in it."

Now was the time to ask. She could not put it off any longer. "Please do not."

He raised an eyebrow and grinned. "How very strange. A woman who doesn't want diamonds. Do not worry, my dear. I can well afford them."

"I know that. I only meant— Robert, I would rather have the money. For this project I have in mind."

He kissed her chin. "What sort of project is that?"

She must do this right. It meant so much to her. "I want to open a shelter. For homeless dogs and cats."

His expression of surprise would have been amusing had she not been so concerned. The hours she had spent thinking and planning had made the shelter very real for her. She wanted it.

She wanted it as she had never wanted anything except her homeplace.

Finally he spoke. "My love, you have a tender heart. And I admire you for it. But, my dear, you cannot save the world."

She managed a little smile. "I don't wish to save the world, Robert. Only a few poor animals."

His fingers moved idly over her arm, traced the curve of her elbow. "Who put this idea into your head?"

"No one. It was mine. Well, Ben came to me this morning." And there in the circle of his arm, she told him the story of the pups. "He was so sweet," she concluded. "He said he wanted to be like you."

Dreyford registered surprise. He had never thought of himself as sweet. "Like me?"

"Yes. You saved Lady Lucky. He wanted to save the pups."

He sighed. "And of course you told him they'd be spared."

Fiona nodded. "Of course. I'll pay for their keep from my pin money."

He frowned. "And this shelter of yours? How do you propose to pay for it?"

She turned pleading eyes on him. "I do not need so many new gowns. And I've plenty of jewels. Oh, please, Robert. I have asked you for very little. Allow me this."

He sighed again. The puppies were no problem, of course. Ben was a good worker and deserved a reward. But this other idea. . . . It was a ridiculous undertaking. The city was full of strays, human as well as animal. To endeavor to help them—

From the rug by the bed came a soft whimper. There was no way Lady could understand what they were talking about—this dog who but for them would have been dead by now. And yet that whimper reached his heart.

Perhaps Fiona was right. Perhaps it was better to do even a little than to do nothing at all.

How they would laugh at him at White's if they knew. Growing soft, they would say. And yet—

"Very well," he told her. "I'll give you an allowance for this addlepated—"

The rest of the sentence was cut off by his wife's kisses. And very satisfying kisses they were, too. It seemed softness had its rewards.

• *Eight* •

Spring turned to summer. With Kitty's help, Fiona found a building on Fleet Street and began getting it in shape. In early July they climbed into Kitty's carriage after an exhausting afternoon there.

Kitty sank down onto the squabs with a weary sigh. "Lord, I am tired. I'd better take a nap when I get home." She made a face. "Imagine! Me taking a nap in midday." She laughed. "I cannot be getting that old. To think that I used to be able to dance all night. By the way, what are you wearing to Lady Heathcote's ball tonight?"

Fiona smiled. "Robert told me to get a new gown, something dazzling." She looked at her friend. "Kitty, I don't want to be dazzling." She grimaced. "The doting mamas all glare at me as it is."

Kitty laughed, bright tinkling laughter that turned the heads of passing gentlemen. "Of course they do. You walked off with the best catch in town."

Fiona smiled. "Yes, I know. Best heart, best hand, best leg. He told me so himself."

"He didn't!" Kitty grinned. "Of course he did. Robbie's never been one to deny his own worth."

"So, what are you wearing?"

Kitty shrugged. "I don't know if we're going. Lately Ginsfield has been feeling so poorly. We never know whether we're going out till the last minute."

"I hope it is nothing serious."

Kitty smiled. "A little too much port is all. It makes his gout act up. Then he's grouchier than a dowager with an ugly daughter. Pain makes my husband positively dragonish."

"Poor Kitty," said Fiona. "I should not like to deal with a dragonish Dreyford."

Kitty stared. "You mean you have not argued? Not yet?"

Remembering the connecting door, Fiona felt herself coloring. "We—we have disagreed about some matters. But we have not really fought."

Kitty shook her head. "I expect it's because you always give way to him. My dear, you must reconsider this. You are setting back the cause of wifehood by such lily-livered behavior."

"But, Kitty, he agreed to the shelter."

Kitty chuckled. "Because he wanted to humor you. But he will not always be so soft. You must stand up for your rights. Believe me, you must. Of course, Dreyford will be a little harder to move than some. But don't you give in. It never pays to let a man have too much power."

Fiona smiled. "Really, Kitty. I can't think why you should give me such contentious advice." She chuckled. "If I did not know you better, I should think you were trying to ruin my marriage."

Kitty laughed. "Now, if I were Roxanne, you might well be suspicious of my motives." She frowned. "Speaking of Roxanne, has she been around lately?"

"No, she has not called again."

The carriage had stopped in front of the house on Grosvenor Square. "Well," said Fiona, stepping down. "Thank you for your help at the shelter. I hope to see you tonight."

Lady Heathcote's ball was a select affair. Only the elite of society were invited. But, Fiona reminded herself, these were people, flesh and blood like any other. Wearing her new tunic gown of pale green over white, edged with a darker green Greek motif, and with the Dreyford emeralds gleaming at her throat, she leaned on the earl's arm.

Kitty was not yet there, but Roxanne had just made a grand entrance in a gown of silver lamé cut so low that every gentleman she passed found his eyes inevitably drawn to its neckline. She moved with the sinuous grace of a serpent, touching a sleeve here, a lapel there, leaving behind her a trail of smiling husbands and seething wives.

She came toward Fiona and the earl, her red mouth forming a seductive smile. "Lovely party, isn't it, milord?" she said, reaching a white-gloved hand toward Dreyford's sleeve.

Fiona pulled his arm away, tucked it through hers. "Yes," she said. "A lovely party. Robert," she continued sweetly, "I believe Lady Jersey is motioning to us."

Lady Jersey had not gestured to them, of course. But she was pleased to see Dreyford approach her, as any woman would be. And while the two of them chatted, Fiona caught her breath and looked around.

Not five feet away stood a dowager whose ostrich plumes waved madly above a bright purple turban and whose bosom sported enough diamonds to float a small navy. Over there were two more of the patronesses from Almack's, cozily chatting, and deciding which people to allow into their choice establishment and which to exclude.

And crossing the room came Lord Byron himself, clad in very broad trousers, to hide his deformed foot no doubt, black coat and waistcoat, and a narrow white cravat. Up close he was even more attractive. With those beautiful black curls and dark soulful eyes he was a man to turn a woman's head. And he obviously knew it.

Still, Dreyford was more handsome. Actually, Dreyford was better-looking than any man in the room. And his clothes were superb. His corbeau-colored coat and breeches were spotless and wrinkle-free. His cravat was shining white and intricately tied. He was the epitome of Beau Brummell's well-dressed gentleman. And she was his wife. She could not quite forgo a feeling of intense satisfaction. She had married the man all London had been after. Why shouldn't she be glad about it?

While she was congratulating herself, a wisp of

a girl paused in the doorway and stood gazing at Byron. Her eyes were huge, rimmed by dark circles and set in a small heart-shaped face that even among these powdered ladies looked pale. Short hair curling around her face gave her a curiously boyish look. And a white muslin gown that on Roxanne would have been shocking, on this young woman only made her look like a sad little girl playing at grown-ups.

At Fiona's side the earl groaned. "Oh, no. Why did *she* come?"

Fiona turned. "Dreyford, what is it?"

"Caro Lamb's here. I certainly hope she behaves."

His choice of words seemed strange. Why shouldn't a lady behave?

But Caro Lamb moved on, away from Byron, and Fiona, looking about for Kitty, ceased to think about the scandalous pair.

She and Dreyford had reached the dining room door when a cry rang out behind them. They turned, of course, but because of the press of people, they could see nothing.

"Wait here," Dreyford said, but she shook her head. So when he made his way back into the other room, she was at his side.

"My God!" Dreyford cried. "The woman is mad. What a thing to do."

Fiona's hand went to her mouth. There on Lady Heathcote's elegant Persian carpet lay an unconscious Caro Lamb. Drops of crimson stained her white gown. By her side knelt several men. But Lord Byron was not among them.

While the men used napkins to staunch the blood welling from Caro's limp white wrists, Byron stood alone, his face whiter than his gleaming cravat. "She broke the glass," he was saying to anyone who would listen. "Broke it and cut her wrists."

"You poor man." Roxanne rushed to his side. "What a horrible thing for you."

For him! Any sympathy Fiona might have felt for the man was instantly obliterated. How could Roxanne be so heartless! And Lord Byron! The woman who loved him was lying unconscious on the carpet and he was lapping up that harpy's sympathy.

With a murmur of disgust Fiona dropped Dreyford's arm and hurried to Caro's side. Heedless of her new gown, she knelt to take the frail body into her arms. "Here now," she soothed, comforting this young woman as she might have comforted a distraught Constance. "It will be all right."

Caro's eyelids flickered and opened. Such a look of gratitude was in those eyes. Fiona felt the tears coming and blinked them back. Caro's lips formed a word. Fiona bent to hear it. "Stay," the lost soul pleaded. "Stay—with—me."

"Do not worry," Fiona reassured her. "I shall stay as long as you need me."

Just then Dreyford reached her side. She felt his hand on her shoulder, heavy with disapproval. And his voice held the same. "Fiona, come. Leave her to the others."

She shook her head. "Robert, I cannot. Let me stay with her till the physician comes. Please."

He frowned. "Fiona, this is not seemly. Can't you see? No other women have come to her aid. You must listen."

Fiona wanted to please him. And it was true, the other women in the room were all busily occupying themselves with something besides the stricken young wife. These men were obviously competent. Maybe she should . . .

From across the room came Roxanne's dulcet tones. "Yes, of course, that's Dreyford's countess. She must be excused. First it was homeless dogs. Can you imagine? And now it's Caro Lamb. But then, poor Fiona's from the country. She doesn't know any better."

Fiona, who had been about to rise in response to Dreyford's look, clasped the injured young woman more tightly to her. "I cannot leave her," she whispered fiercely. "She needs me."

Dreyford swallowed a curse. These society people could not understand such tenderheartedness. In a twisted way Roxanne was right. By her kindness Fiona was making herself a laughing stock.

Her eyes pleaded with him. And in that instant he realized that scandal and gossip meant nothing to her. In Caro Lamb she saw simply a creature in pain.

But he didn't want his wife comforting this woman. Caro's ideas were too farfetched, never mind that she got them from William. A woman could not behave as a man did, running about freely, taking whomever she chose. It set a bad example. It was—it was indecent.

He spied Kitty crossing the room toward him and moved to meet her.

"Quite a spectacle," she said, smiling at him.

He frowned. "Yes, and my wife has to rush to the rescue."

Kitty chuckled. "It must run in the family. And she has infected me, as you know. But of course you started it."

As always, Kitty could make him smile, though this time ruefully. "I know," he said. "But who would have thought it would lead to this? Kitty, please, get my wife to give this thing up. You know Caro can't be good for her."

She patted his hand. "I'll do my best. But Robbie, Fiona has a good heart. And you know, good-hearted people are the hardest to move."

"I have confidence in you."

She grimaced. "Let us hope it is not ill placed."

Fiona saw her husband and Kitty exchange looks. Why couldn't the man understand about love? Caro Lamb, for all her infamous reputation, was still a human being. It could not be easy to be rejected by the man you loved, to be laughed at and insulted by people who were no better, and might certainly be worse, than you.

Caro moaned and Fiona leaned closer. "What is it, dear?"

"I love him so. But he . . ." And two great tears trickled down Caro's pale cheeks to stain the front of her already ruined gown.

Fiona said the first thing that came to mind. "He's not worth it."

"Oh, but he is! He is worth . . . everything."

Yes, Fiona thought. She remembered how Lonigan had been everything to her. But Lonigan had been a good man. About Lord Byron she had her doubts, especially as he was now standing across the room, conversing with Roxanne as though nothing untoward had even happened.

Caro fell silent then. William Lamb came up, his eyes grave. "Thank you," he said to Fiona. "It was kind of you to help. The carriage will be out front now. I'll take my wife home."

When her husband lifted her, Caro opened her eyes once more. "Come . . . see me," she whispered.

"Yes, yes, I shall. I promise."

Fiona stood up, her heart in her throat, unshed tears in her eyes. Caro's husband seemed to love her. Yet Caro's love was given to Byron, who did not love her. What a tangle life was. Why couldn't the right people love each other?

"Fiona."

She turned and there stood her friend. "Kitty, I see you got here."

Kitty nodded. "But evidently not in time for all the excitement."

"The poor thing. She loves him so."

Kitty frowned. "There are many kinds of love. Some are more destructive than others."

"Perhaps. But love should always be respected. It is so important."

Kitty sighed. "And what of marriage vows?"

That was not a matter Fiona cared to discuss. She changed the subject. "I like her," she said, knowing Kitty would raise an eyebrow. "She goes after what she wants."

Kitty shook her head. "She should have listened to herself."

"What do you mean?"

"When she first met him, Caro said Byron was mad, bad, and dangerous to know. And she was right."

"He certainly did not do anything to help her tonight. And did you hear Roxanne?"

Kitty shrugged. "Forget Roxanne. Why *should* Byron get involved? He has made it quite clear that their affair is over. Caro is behaving stupidly, chasing after a man who no longer wants her." Kitty sniffed disdainfully. "I should have more pride than that. You'd better not see her again. She's bad business all around."

Kitty was probably right. Still, Fiona asked, "Where does she live?"

Kitty frowned. "In Melbourne House with his people. Why?"

"Because I mean to go round tomorrow to see how she is."

Kitty's frown deepened. "Fiona, Dreyford will not like this. He will not like it one little bit."

"I know. But it's no use, Kitty. This is where I take my stand."

"But that is foolishness. I did not mean anything like this."

Fiona smiled. "I know. But I do mean it. And no one can stop me."

"Perhaps not," said Kitty with a sigh. "But I will tell you this. You are making a huge mistake."

By the next afternoon Fiona was not so sure she should disregard Kitty's advice. After all, Kitty did know a lot more about the world of the ton than she did. But she was genuinely worried about Caro Lamb and so, taking her meager courage in her hands, she ordered the carriage and set out.

Melbourne House was quite imposing, but she did not allow herself time to admire the architecture. She descended from the carriage and went immediately to the front door.

The butler was imposing, too, but he softened when she gave her name. "She'll be glad to see a friendly face," he whispered, before his own face reset into its stern mask. "Up those stairs, Lady Dreyford."

Caro was lying on the couch. She held a novel in one hand and a half-eaten chocolate in the other. "Oh, do come in," she cried. "It will be lovely to have someone to talk to. Mama and William have been positively fierce. Take off your bonnet and stay awhile. Do."

Fiona took a chair and removed her bonnet. She had expected a pale weak invalid, scarcely able to speak, and here was Caro, devouring chocolates.

"Help yourself," Caro said, indicating the box. "They're passable." She smiled and her face became younger, softer. "You were so kind to me last night, Fiona. Everyone else . . ."

She waved a hand and Fiona winced at the sight of her bandaged wrist.

"Everyone else kept yammering about my foolishness." And then to Fiona's complete surprise, Caro Lamb actually grinned. "They are the fools, not to value love."

"But—" Fiona did not quite know how to talk to this fey creature. "But if he doesn't love you . . ."

Caro's face darkened. "He loves me. He'll remember how it was with us. He's—he's a strange man. Secretive. Scarred."

"His clubfoot—"

"No, no!" Caro waved a hand impatiently. "Not scars on his body. Scars on his mind. His childhood . . . his sister . . ." She sighed. "He has suffered and so he makes others suffer."

Fiona wished to dispute the sense of such actions. Surely suffering need not be compounded in this awful fashion. But Caro's eyes were growing wilder, her gestures more violent. "Tell me," Fiona said. "Did you really mean to—to—"

"To kill myself?" Caro's innocent expression was in such contrast to her words that Fiona shivered. "I don't really know. I did not plan it out ahead, if that's what you mean. I just wanted to see him. To talk to him. But he didn't want— He wouldn't even—" She stopped and rubbed at her eyes. "But he will change his mind. He has to."

She leaned forward. "But, please, let us talk about you. So you're married to Dreyford."

"Yes, to Dreyford."

Caro shook her head. "Marriage, marriage is not all they say it is. I thought— William and I were so happy. And then, then . . ."

Her eyes filled with tears again and Fiona hurried to change the subject. "I—I believe I will try one of those chocolates after all. Where did you get them?"

Caro smiled. "Mama had them sent. Mama is good to me. So is William, really, I—I just . . ."

Again the tears threatened, and Fiona hastened to ask, "What are you reading today?"

"A novel. William brought it to me. It is very good. The heroine loves so madly, so passionately. And the hero . . . the hero is like my Byron. They will get together at the end. As we will."

Fiona could think of no reply to make to this. The Byron she had seen clearly did not feel as Caro did. If once he had loved her passionately, madly—and given his reputation Fiona had no reason to doubt it—he certainly no longer harbored such feelings. For Lord Byron, this affair was over.

After another hour during which Caro recounted the entire history of her tumultuous relationship with the poet, Fiona took her departure. It was clear to her that Caro Lamb was badly in need of a friend. And in spite of all her problems, her wildness, and her shocking behavior, there was about her a sort of strange innocence, a childishness that Fiona found intriguing.

* * *

Fiona stepped into the front hall of the house on Grosvenor Square just as the earl gave his curly-brimmed beaver to Berkins and bent to scratch behind the eager dog's ears. "Hello," he said. "Out making calls?"

She pulled off a glove. "Ye-es." She had not meant to hesitate, but she had never been good at lying.

"Hear any interesting *on dits*?"

"Not really." She knew she was not putting a good face on it.

The earl straightened. "Fiona, please come into the library with me. We have a matter that needs discussing."

"Yes, milord." She gave her bonnet and gloves to Berkins and followed her husband into the library. The dog, of course, went too.

The earl pointed to a chair. "Sit down, please."

She sat. "What is it, milord?"

He leaned against the mantelpiece, looking every inch the lord and master. "Last night you were tired, distraught. I did not wish to disturb you further. So I waited till today to discuss this rather distressing matter."

Indeed, he had not disturbed her at all, but left her lying all night alone, waiting for his coming. She sat silent, knowing there was more to be said. Knowing, too, that she did not want to hear it.

"It was Christian of you to go to Caro Lamb's assistance that way." He straightened. "You have a kind nature. But you must take care."

He paused, and since he seemed to be waiting, she asked, "How so, milord?"

He frowned. "Caro Lamb is not a fit friend for a woman of your position."

Deliberately she misunderstood him. "She is a lady. The wife of a lord. How can she not be fit?"

"Fiona!" The thundered word sent Lady whimpering under the couch. But Fiona refused to cower. "Yes, milord?"

He took a deep breath. "You know quite well what I mean. Caro Lamb is the object of much gossip. Her immoral alliance with Byron . . ."

She felt compelled to tell him. "Milord, she said they have never even—"

His eyebrows met in a frown so fierce the dog whimpered again. "Such things should not be on a lady's tongue."

Now he was being ridiculous. "May I remind you that *I* did not bring up the subject. It was you who said she is not fit."

"And she is not."

"Because she loves Byron."

"Yes."

"I daresay there are many young women in London who fancy themselves in love with Lord Byron. Am I to be forbidden the company of them all?"

"Fi—" He stopped and glanced at the dog. When he spoke again, his tone was more moderate. "Must you bait me like this? My concern is only for you. If your name is connected with Caro Lamb's you will become as infamous as she. I do not want my lady to be talked about."

There it was. His real concern was for his reputation. "Of course not," she said icily. "But might I suggest that if people talk, it will be about you."

Dreyford smacked one fist into the other and winced. Why must she be so contrary? He tried counting to ten. But the Dreyford temper, once unleashed, was difficult to contain. "Of course they will talk about me, for permitting such an affiliation."

She stared back at him, her eyes cold. "That is not what I meant."

Again he had to count. This fractious creature would drive him to insanity yet. "Then what *do* you mean?"

She faced him squarely, her chin up. "I mean that *I* may not befriend poor Caro Lamb. A woman whose worst sin is that she loves a man who does not return her love. But *you* may continue your liaison with the Lady Roxanne."

Her eyes were fierce now. Did that mean she was jealous? To his surprise he found the idea rather satisfying. "You have been misinformed," he said sharply. "I have no liaison with Roxanne. Nor have I had one since you and I were wed."

From the look on her face, she did not believe him. "Your suspicions are entirely unfounded," he continued. "But even if they were not, the comparison is inapplicable."

Her eyes grew even fiercer. "Indeed. I suppose now you will tell me that men and women must comport themselves by different standards."

That seemed obvious enough to him. "Of course."

"And why is that?"

He shrugged. "It has always been so."

She smiled, as an India tiger might smile before making a meal of a plump native. "I see. So a long history makes injustice permissible."

He had little patience left. "Of course not."

"But you just said—"

"Forget what I said!" There he went again, thundering like some deranged potentate. Why did she make him so irrational? "That is—" He modulated his tone. "I do not wish to discuss this any further. It only upsets you and—"

"*I* am not upset, milord."

He refrained from kicking the fireplace fender. But only barely. What was worse, she was right. He was rapidly losing face. He pulled in another deep breath and made a supreme effort to be calm. "You are right," he said. "I am upset. And consequently I am not doing this as well as I might wish. But regardless of that I mean to say something. I think it extremely dangerous for you to pursue your friendship with Caro Lamb. So I am asking you to discontinue it, to give me your word that you will not see her again."

He had done it poorly. And from the look on her face, he had utterly failed in his intent.

"I am sorry," she said, head up, voice steady. "But I cannot in good conscience do such a thing. I do not desert my friends when they need me."

For a moment he considered making his request into a command. But from the look of her a command would be wasted. He sighed. "Very well,

I believe we have nothing more to say to each other."

Fiona watched him stalk out, the dog at his heels. And then, only then, did she let herself relax. She had angered him dreadfully. But she could not turn her back on her loyalties and still feel like a decent human being.

With a sigh she rose from her seat and turned toward the stairs. It was going to be a long and lonely night.

• *Nine* •

A WEEK WENT by, a long difficult week in which the words exchanged by Fiona and Dreyford could be counted on the fingers of two hands.

She did not refrain from seeing Caro Lamb, but she kept her visits discreet, not mentioning them during her other calls. And before too long Caro announced that her mother was taking her to the country to recuperate.

A day or so after their departure Dreyford looked up from the breakfast table to announce rather diffidently, "Don't forget, my dear. We're expected at the Jerseys' soiree tonight. It would please me if you wore the peach silk."

And so that afternoon as the carriage approached the shelter on Fleet Street, she reported to Kitty. "He's speaking to me again. I suppose it's because Caro and her mother have left town."

"Thank goodness." Kitty frowned. "I cannot understand how you could defy him so flagrantly."

Fiona looked at her friend. "But you yourself suggested—"

"Not in something like this. Not where your reputation is concerned."

Fiona swallowed a sigh. She dearly loved Kitty, but sometimes she was hard put to understand her. "It was a matter of principle, you see. I could not turn my back on a friend."

"Friend?" Kitty raised an eyebrow. "Caro would turn her back on you. Faster even than Byron did on her."

Perhaps Kitty was right. Still, that did not alter matters. "I cannot help that. I had to do what I thought was right."

Kitty shook her head. "And you were not afraid for the shelter?"

For a moment Fiona did not take her friend's meaning. When she understood the question, she sent Kitty an accusing look. "Of course not. Dreyford would not do something like that. He's not a petty man."

Kitty patted her hand. "You're quite right, my dear. He is not petty at all. And lucky for you." She adjusted her bonnet and smiled. "So, enough of that. Tell me, have you had any success finding someone to run the place?"

Fiona sighed. "No. And it's been quite difficult. It must be someone who truly loves animals, you know. And so far . . ." She frowned. "Many people have come in. But none of them will suit. I have some more interviews this afternoon. Perhaps one of them will do."

Kitty nodded. "I truly never thought we'd get this far. Just think, next week the shelter will be ready to open."

"Yes. Ben is so excited. He's been down almost every day to see how things are going."

The carriage stopped and the two climbed down. "Better give us three hours," Fiona told Huggins.

"Yes, milady."

She stood there for a moment, surveying the building. It didn't look like much: a dirty, run-down structure on a street that teemed with the worst dregs of humanity. But next week this nondescript building would house her dream come true.

"Oh, Kitty, I am so pleased!"

"And I. But you'd best get ready for your interviews. You must find someone to run the place." Kitty grinned. "I'm quite sure Robbie would draw the line at your doing *that* yourself!"

Laughing together, they went inside.

Several hours later, Fiona leaned back in her chair and sighed. The interviews had not been going well. Person after person had told her how much he loved animals. But there was something off-putting about each of them. And in this so important matter she had only her instincts to trust.

Then Mr. Hadley arrived, a little man with a big smile and a voice like gravel.

"Me and the missus," he said with a grin, "we got these two dogs and three cats. Ain't got no little 'uns, you see. So we got dogs and cats instead. We'd have more of 'em if we had room. The missus, she pure loves 'em."

Fiona asked him some more questions. And every answer confirmed her feelings. Here—at last—was the man for the job.

She told him so. "I want you and Mrs. Hadley to live on the premises. To give the animals a real home."

Mr. Hadley grinned. "The missus ain't gonna believe it. Us having all them animals." He frowned. "But what about our own?"

"You'll bring them with you, of course."

Smiling and nodding, Mr. Hadley finally backed from the room.

Propping her elbows on the table, Fiona let her head sink into her hands. She was elated to have finally found someone to run the shelter. And she was pleased that things with Dreyford were getting back to normal. But she was so tired. Their confrontation over Caro Lamb had taken its toll on her.

She heard the creak of the opening door. "Kitty, I think—"

But it was not Kitty. It was. . . . It couldn't be, but it was. The man who stood there was Lonigan.

She stared at him, hardly able to believe her eyes.

He stared back at her. "Fiona! Is it truly you, me darling?"

"Yes. I— You're alive!" What a stupid thing to say. But her heart was pounding so, she could hardly think.

He grinned. "That I am, lass. Alive and kicking. Did ye think otherwise?"

"I—" Her tongue didn't want to work properly and her mind seemed dazed. "When you didn't come home, I thought—"

"You thought I'd kicked off. No, no, me darling. I was pressed. Into the navy. That's why I vanished the way I did."

She nodded. All these years she had hoped—prayed—to see him alive again. And now that he was here, standing before her, she didn't know what to do, what to say.

His glance took in her expensive walking dress. His grin broadened. "Ye've come up in the world, I see. What Lord has the keeping of ye now?"

"Keeping?" For some reason she did not mention her marriage. "Oh, ah, you wouldn't know him."

Lonigan grinned. "A young pup, huh? Well, bully for you."

She tried to get her thoughts in order, to make sense out of this. "Why, why are you here?"

He hooked his thumbs in his waistcoat, a gaudy affair shot with gold thread and showing considerable wear. "I seen an advertisement. To run some kind of shelter. So here I am."

For a moment in her shock she'd forgotten all about the shelter. "Oh, yes. I'm sorry. That position's been filled."

He shrugged. "Ah, well. 'Tis still me lucky day. I'll just—"

"Fiona." Tying her bonnet strings, Kitty came hurrying through the door. "I'm sorry to bother you, but I really must leave. Ginsfield gets positively bearish when I'm late." Her eyes widened as she saw the stranger standing there.

"This is Mr. Lonigan," Fiona explained, trying to behave normally. "I was just telling him that

Mr. Hadley's already been given the position we advertised." She turned to the man who had once been her husband. "I'm sorry to rush you, sir. But we must be on our way."

"Of course." He bowed to them with a flourish. "Till we meet again, ladies."

Kitty stared after him. "A strange man. Looks almost like a gentleman. One of those Irish fortune hunters, no doubt."

Fiona nodded. Her heart was pounding in her throat. She had to get home, to think, to understand what this all meant. "Come, let's go. We don't want to make Ginsfield bearish."

Later, in the privacy of her room, Fiona sank down on the chaise longue. Lonigan was alive! Moments ago he'd been standing right there in front of her.

But she felt no joy, no elation. She felt— She put a hand to her trembling mouth. She felt a terrible anxiety.

If Lonigan was really, legally, her husband, she did not belong here, in this house that belonged to the Earl of Dreyford. And what of Dreyford? If he knew, what would he say? What would he do?

Her thoughts raced as she tried to remember how Lonigan had acted, what he had said to her. But her memory was blurred, overlaid with the haze of anxiety. She tried to reconcile the man she had seen with the memory she'd carried these many years. The way he dressed and carried himself, qualities she had once so admired, now seemed cheap and pretentious. The voice that had once thrilled her now rang insincerely in her ears. And his smile—the smile she had remembered for so long—was now a false and fulsome thing.

Tears rose to her eyes. All these years she'd been loving a dream, a pretty dream of her own devising. Whatever she had felt for Lonigan no longer existed. It had died long ago.

He might once have been her husband, the center of her life. But now—she bit her bottom lip as she recognized the fearful truth—her body, her heart, belonged to Dreyford.

But her husband did not love her. He did not believe in love. And if he discovered the truth. . . . She could not think about that.

She rose and washed her face. Perhaps she was being foolish. At any rate, she must go on as usual. It was time to dress for the soiree.

That evening, wearing the peach satin and the Dreyford emeralds, she gazed around her. Lady Jersey's dining room held a dazzling collection of society's notables. If only she could get some of these people to help with the shelter. But several grand dames had already looked down their aristocratic noses and sniffed at the suggestion that they might want to help. They would rather squander their money on more useless gowns and jewels.

But then, what could she expect? In a city where babies were regularly abandoned, who would think to care about animals?

Across the beautifully laid table Lord Byron

chuckled. He did not look at all downcast, this man who had ruined Caro Lamb's life.

Fiona's heart skipped a beat. The scandal about Caro had been on everyone's tongue for weeks. But that would be nothing compared to the furor that would be aroused if it were discovered that she and Dreyford were not legally married.

She must stop this kind of thinking. Lonigan might intend nothing. He might already have left the city. She might never see him again. There was no use in borrowing trouble.

Besides, there was trouble already in the room. Roxanne had been seated on Byron's right. And Roxanne was her usual seductive self, leaning toward the poet in a manner that allowed the bosom of her gown to fall away.

Fiona sighed. Poor Caro had definitely made a mistake in loving this man. There he sat, laughing and joking with Roxanne as though Caro Lamb had never meant a thing to him. And perhaps she hadn't. But Caro was so sure she had.

At least in her own case, she had that advantage. If such it could be called. She knew that her husband did not love her. He had been very clear on that point. But at least he did not love anyone else. And there lay her hope.

Dreyford sat on Roxanne's other side. He was close enough for Fiona to see, but too far away to converse with. It was a deplorable habit of hostesses, Fiona felt, the seating of husbands and wives so far apart. She wished he were by her side. Even silent he was better company than the foppish Phillipe de Noir who sat on her left. De

Noir made another inane remark and she smiled blankly and nodded.

And then Roxanne laughed. The sound made Fiona look up from her roast pheasant. Roxanne's words carried easily across the table. "Oh, my dear George," she simpered, "you are too amusing."

Lord Byron smiled. "I assure you. It is true."

Roxanne's laughter shrilled out. "Oh, silly boy, you can't mean it."

"Indeed I do."

Lady Jersey looked up from her plate. "Come, Roxanne. You must share your little joke with the rest of us."

To Fiona's surprise, Byron began to look a trifle embarrassed. But Roxanne apparently felt no constraint. She looked around the table, intent on an audience. "He was just telling me all the things she did. Following him around in that page's outfit. And sending him love letters. And hair from—" Dreyford coughed and Roxanne stopped in midsentence.

But she recovered herself quickly and went on. "Imagine a woman going about dressed as a page. And look what she did at Lady Heathcote's ball. It's scandalous for a lady to behave so." Roxanne's red lips pursed in a pout. "Her husband ought to go to Parliament and get a writ of divorce."

The room grew silent. Across the table from Fiona, Byron suddenly found his pheasant of great interest. Others, too, focused their attention on their plates. No one said anything. No one offered one word in defense of poor Caro Lamb.

And Fiona's hackles went up. "Perhaps," she said, and the words fell into the silence like little cannon shells exploding, "perhaps her husband loves her."

A glance at Dreyford showed him frowning fiercely. She would hear about this later. But at the moment she didn't care. She hurried on. "Some husbands do, you know, love their wives." Her eyes met Roxanne's. "But of course you cannot be expected to understand that. The only husbands you know belong to other women."

Dreyford's look grew even darker. Roxanne paled and turned to him, putting a possessive hand on his sleeve. "At least I should not leave my husband while I ran around after stray curs." She raised an eyebrow. "Or have you some *other* reason for your excursions to Fleet Street?"

A picture of Lonigan flashed into Fiona's mind. But Roxanne could not possibly know about him. "I want to do something helpful in this world," Fiona said. "But I cannot expect you to understand compassion, either, since I doubt you have ever in your life experienced it."

Lady Jersey made a moue of distaste. She did not approve of such altercations at her dinner table. "Dear Roxanne," she said, with a quelling glance in Fiona's direction, "you must tell me where you got that marvelous gown."

Swallowing a sigh, Fiona subsided. There was little point in saying more, she thought, pushing the food around her plate. These people—people like Roxanne—did not know how to think of anyone but themselves. No one would take Caro's side. They were all intent on lionizing Byron, that pretty poet.

And now she had angered Dreyford again, just when she should be on her best behavior. And that catty remark of Roxanne's would linger in his mind. If he did find out about Lonigan, he would come to an entirely wrong conclusion. Oh, why had she let that woman irritate her so?

There was no answer to that question or to the others that plagued her throughout the long and difficult evening. She understood that they could not leave immediately after dinner. Certainly she didn't fancy giving the impression she'd been dragged away in disgrace. But to stay until almost everyone else had gone, that thought pushed her already taut nerves almost to the breaking point.

Still, she managed, smiling and chatting until finally, mercifully, they had made their farewells and her husband handed her into the carriage.

"I know I embarrassed you," she said into the silence as the coach pulled away. "I'm sorry for that. Though not for what I said." She sighed. This silence of his was almost worse than being shouted at.

"I do not understand the ways of the ton," she went on. "Surely Roxanne is worse than Caro Lamb. Roxanne deliberately entices other women's husbands. Sometimes I think she does it just for the sport of it."

In the light of the carriage lamps Dreyford looked fierce, but she pushed on. "Caro *loves*

Byron. I know, milord, you do not believe in love. But why is love more scandalous than—than, say, dalliance? Why does Lady Jersey invite Byron and not Caro? Was he not equally guilty in the matter? And look, Lady Jersey seats you beside Roxanne. She sees nothing wrong with putting you next to your former inamorata."

Watching her, Dreyford swallowed a sigh. She was making life difficult for them both with her defense of the little Lamb. He should be very angry. He was, in sober fact, quite disturbed by tonight's fiasco. It would echo through the ton for days to come. And they did not need that sort of attention.

But he was also aware of something else. He realized that he admired his wife's courage. She was foolish, of course. Probably wrong. But where she believed, she stood firm. She was a good friend, a loyal friend.

But all her impassioned defenses of the Lamb, or of love, would change nothing. The ton had its own values. And love, compassion, and loyalty counted for very little with them. Yes, they would be talking about her again, especially about that remark of Roxanne's concerning Fleet Street.

He sighed. He had never liked his wife going into such a neighborhood. Huggins had strict instructions to stay close, to keep an eye on things.

He had not, of course, told the coachman to report on her visitors there. And he would not. These were the musings of a jealous husband. Not the sort of thing he would do.

Besides, to suspect Fiona of unfaithfulness was the outside of foolishness.

She was staring at him, plainly waiting for his temper to explode. Assuredly, he was not a man of great patience. He had handled the whole Caro Lamb affair in the worst possible fashion. And now. . . . Here was a second chance.

"Please—" There was the slightest quaver in her voice. "Please, Dreyford, shout at me. Shout at me and get it over with. I know you think I deserve it. Perhaps I do. But please, just shout. Then talk to me again."

She sat there, braced upright, waiting for him to pummel her with his words. And suddenly he found that he had no need to restrain his temper. He concluded, almost to his surprise, that he was not angry with his wife.

"What you did was foolish," he said. "But I am not angry."

She gaped at him. "You're not?"

"No, my dear. You were being loyal to your friend."

"But you said—"

"I don't agree with you, of course," he continued. "Because I think the little Lamb, in her own way, is just as willful as Roxanne. But I believe I can see your point."

Plainly she did not believe him. "Yes, well—"

"I spent the evening by your side, didn't I?"

Her mouth twisted. "Yes. But there was your reputation to consider."

He did not dispute that. "Quite true. But I have been dragged through the mud before. And, I assure you, it is not a pleasant experience. I should like to have you spared such an ordeal."

Clearly she did not know how to respond to this unusual turn of events. He didn't wait for her to come up with more arguments, but moved swiftly over to the squabs beside her. "I admire loyalty," he said softly. "And I practice it myself."

Up close he could see there were tears in her eyes. He pulled her to him and kissed them away. "Forget the ton," he said, slipping his arm around her. "Forget Caro Lamb. Think only of us."

• *Ten* •

For several days Fiona expected Lonigan to show up at any moment. Things were once again right between her and Dreyford, and she did all she could to keep them that way, making no mention of Caro Lamb to anyone. But the memory of Lonigan was always there. Would he appear at the shelter again?

Still, when the days passed with no word from him, she began to think that Cousin Charles had for once been right. Their marriage had been a sham and Lonigan had no claim on her. She wanted desperately to believe that, but somehow she could not quite convince herself.

In the meantime she poured all her energies into the work for the shelter. Even when she wrote to Caro at her mother's country house, the letter was full of the shelter. Seeing this, she appended a note suggesting that on her return Caro might want to help with the work there.

The shelter was set to open on Monday next but Fiona had the Hadleys and their menagerie moved in on Friday. That afternoon she came home, weary and satisfied, after seeing them settled. Ben, considerably cleaner now that she'd insisted he bathe every day, perched on the velvet squabs across from her, chattering happily about his puppies. "And I been doing me job," he said proudly. "They all knows about it."

"They?" Fiona said absently, her mind on other matters.

Ben's mouth turned down. "Them what lives around there. I told 'em all. And they'll tell others."

Of course. She smiled at him. "You're a good boy, Ben. You know, without you there wouldn't have been any shelter."

The child's face turned red. "Oh, no, me lady. It was your idea."

"Let's share the credit, then," she said, wishing she could be more enthusiastic. She was just so tired. She'd been driving herself every moment. And she knew it was not just to get the shelter ready on time. At least when she was busy there, she could keep Lonigan out of her mind.

They reached the house and Ben smiled at her. "Will you be coming out to the stable to see the pups?"

She was bone weary, but the boy's eagerness tugged at her heart. "Yes, Ben. Of course."

Half an hour later, she was climbing the back stairs. She wanted a bath and a night of uninterrupted sleep, both rather unlikely at the moment. When she emerged in the upper hallway, Millie turned from her dusting. "Oh, milady. There you are. You had a caller this afternoon. And a pretty fine gentleman he was."

Fiona's heart hit the roof of her mouth and plummeted to the pit of her stomach. "Did he leave his name?"

Millie flushed. "I didn't hear it, milady. I was doing the hall here and I peeked over the banister to see if it was you coming home."

Fiona nodded. "Very well, Millie."

Wearily she turned away. In her bones she felt that it was Lonigan and he would return. If only she had some way to stop him. But first she'd have to see what he wanted.

She washed and went down to the drawing room. A quick inquiry to Berkins told her the gentleman had left no card. But he had said he would be back soon. She had expected that. Patience had never been one of Lonigan's better qualities.

She picked up her needlework, then put it down again with an exclamation of disgust. How could she think about stitching when her whole life hung in the balance? Her heart jumped a beat. Not just *her* life, but the shelter's very existence, depended on Lonigan and what he decided to do.

Finally, when she thought she could stand it no longer, Berkins stood in the doorway. The slightest hint of distaste crossed his usually expressionless face. "A Mr. Lonigan, milady. To see you."

"Show him in, please, Berkins." She tried to compose her features. She must look as though this were merely a social visit.

Lonigan sauntered in, smiling cheerfully. "Nice little place ye've got here," he said, settling himself in a chair. "Why didn't ye tell me ye was so well-heeled?"

He didn't wait for an answer. "Letting me think ye was in keeping. And all along ye've got a fancy earl for a husband. Leastways, that's what he thinks. Wonder what he'll say when he hears different."

Her mouth went dry, but she reminded herself to keep calm. "What do you mean? You know we weren't really married."

"Not really married?" He stretched his legs and admired his boots. "Me dear, yer're mistook. We tied the knot, pure and simple. Don't ye remember Brother Andrews? Oh, yes, we're married."

He let his glance rove around the sumptuous room. She could almost see him adding up figures in his mind. So much for the Turner over the mantel. So much for the Constable on that wall.

He gave her a calculating look. "And ye being here is all a mistake. Ye don't belong in this fancy place, me dear. Ye belong with me."

She bit back an exclamation of distaste, and fought to keep her expression serene. How could she ever have thought she loved this man? "Why are you here? What do you want?"

He chuckled. "Always direct, ain't ye, me dear? I'm here cause I need some ready." He looked around the room again. "He'll never miss it, fer sure."

Her worst fears were realized. He meant to blackmail her. "But I haven't any—"

His jovial expression faded. "Then get it. I aim to have my share of all this. 'Tis only right and proper, him having taken me beloved wife from me."

"I'm not—"

His expression hardened. "Now, is that a nice way to be talking to yer husband?"

This was a nightmare. If only she could wake up. "Have you proof?"

He shook his head. "Not with me, I don't." He took out an enameled snuffbox and helped himself to a pinch. "Do ye think I'd be lugging the preacher around with me? Besides, me dear"—he gave her a grin that made her stomach lurch in disgust—"I know ye want to stay here. Who wouldn't? So ye just get me the ready. Do that and ye'll be cozy as a flea." Ostentatiously, he picked a piece of lint off his coat sleeve. "We'll start with a couple hundred pounds."

Her stomach tightened again and she tasted bile. Where could she get that kind of money? "A couple—"

"Aye." He cut her off. "I seen that shelter of yern. I know that fancy earl finances it. Tell him ye need more cash."

What should she do? She tried to think. "It'll take time to get the money. I spent everything I had. And he knows the shelter is ready. I can't ask him for more right now."

Lonigan nodded sagely. "I'm a reasonable man, I am. I'll give ye a week to come up with some emergency. A week. Then I go to that husband of yern." He looked around him. "And all this is gone." He snapped his fingers. "Pouf! Just like that."

She nodded. Anything to get him out of there. "All right. A week. But don't come here anymore. Come to—"

The door opened to admit the earl. A pattern card of perfection in his fawn-colored trousers and coat of blue superfine, he cast a pained look at this intruder unexpectedly lolling in his delicate lyre-back chair.

Fiona forced a smile. If she hung on a little longer, she could carry this off. "Milord, this is Mr. Lonigan. He came to see me about a position in the shelter. I'm afraid I had to tell him it's already filled."

Dreyford did not look pleased at this news. His expression grew more disgruntled.

She got to her feet and Lonigan did the same. "If we have another opening, Mr. Lonigan, we'll be putting it in the *Times.*"

"Aye, milady." Lonigan's attitude was all subservience, but under it she detected the mockery. Still, she knew he would not betray her at the moment. He would give her the week. She swallowed a sigh of relief as he bowed his way out.

Across the room Dreyford leaned against the mantel, his mouth twisted in a grimace of distaste. "I realize that the shelter is important to you, my dear. But in the future please conduct such business down there. I don't like that sort dirtying up my drawing room."

She nodded. "Of course. He was awful, wasn't he?" She hardly knew what she was saying. Her mouth seemed to form words of its own accord. "I'm sorry. Someone must have told him where we live. I'll see that it doesn't happen again. You can be sure of that."

Dreyford felt a stab of apprehension. Why did she rattle on like that? And why were her cheeks so flushed and her eyes so bright?

Good Lord, could Roxanne have possibly been right? Could he have stumbled into a tête-à-tête between his wife and a lover?

For a moment it seemed he couldn't breathe. How could she do such a thing—right there in their home? And with such a down-and-outer? He should go right after him and teach the dog his place.

But common sense asserted itself. Fiona was not stupid, or cruel. If she desired to take a lover, she would find one of better quality than that lout. And she would do it discreetly. She was not the sort to flaunt the fellow in her home.

Somehow this knowledge did little to raise his spirits. He did not want discretion from his wife. He wanted fidelity. He wanted love.

This rather amazing piece of insight made his frown grow fiercer. The woman intruded into all the areas of his life. She *was* his life.

That was impossible. He pushed the thought from him. He did not love his wife. He had sworn never to love a woman again. He merely enjoyed her company.

Fiona spent a sleepless night. Should she have told Dreyford everything? she wondered. How out of her fear of Charles she had deceived him, had not told him about Lonigan? But she did not want to make such a decision without giving it sufficient thought. Such words, once spoken, could never be recalled. And it would be better when she told him to have all the facts.

Her husband lay beside her, his body relaxed in sleep, and she considered what she should do. If only she had told him everything that day in Charles's study. If only she had entered their union with a clean conscience. But she had not. She had kept the truth from her husband-to-be. And now she was going to pay for it.

And so she spent the night in that most useless of pastimes: considering what might have been. And sometime just before dawn she decided what it was she must do. First, she would find out if Lonigan really had any proof of their marriage. The more she saw of him, the more unlikely it seemed that he would actually have married a poor relation. And he couldn't have known about the dowry or he would have claimed it immediately.

So, after she looked into the matter of proof, she would decide what to do next. And finally she slept.

When she arrived at Kitty's at noon, her friend looked up from her needlepoint and clucked a sympathetic tongue. "My word, Fiona. Do sit down. You look positively haggard. Whatever is wrong?"

Now that she was there, she didn't know what to do, what to say. "I—I heard the most dreadful story. From a friend of mine."

Kitty's brows knit in a frown. "Tell me."

"She was married once. Very young. Or thought she was. The man disappeared. Years later she married another." She swallowed. She could not let Kitty see how this upset her. "And then the man came back."

The usually imperturbable Kitty gasped. "And now she has *two* husbands?"

Fiona nodded. "*If* the first marriage was legal. He says it was. And he—he wants money to keep his secret."

Kitty's eyes narrowed. "And what does she think you can do?"

"They were married near Fleet Street. I—I have the name of the man who married them. She thought—I thought perhaps you would help me look for him."

Kitty raised her hands in a gesture of supplication. "Fiona, you know how it is down there. We shall never find anything."

"I know." She was very much afraid Kitty was right. But she had to do something. If she could prove Lonigan was lying, she could pull his teeth. "But I must try. Will you help me?"

Kitty's frown grew worse. "Your friend should go to her husband. Tell him the truth. Throw herself on his mercy. If he loves her . . ."

Fiona swallowed a sob. "He doesn't, though. And she's afraid. Because she loves him."

"Oh, Fiona!"

She could not look at Kitty. Her friend's sympathy would reduce her to tears and this was a secret she could not share. "Will you help me?"

Kitty got to her feet. "Of course. Just let me get my bonnet."

Fleet Street was a jumbled mass of humanity, most of it none too clean. Fiona, with Kitty beside her and a worried Huggins trailing along behind, made inquiries at every establishment. But nobody had heard of Brother Andrews. And when she said that seven years had passed, they only shook their heads.

Six days they spent—long, weary, and utterly unproductive days of seeking. But Brother Andrews—if such he had really been—had disappeared from the face of the earth.

On the afternoon of the sixth day they collapsed into the carriage. "It's no use," Fiona said. "We'll never find him."

Kitty cast a sympathetic glance. "Fiona, we'll keep looking."

Fiona shook her head. "We can't. The week's up."

"I don't understand."

"He only gave m—her a week. He'll be coming for the money. And she doesn't have it." Her voice threatened to break and she bit down hard on her bottom lip to stop its trembling. She could not be seen crying in a carriage on Fleet Street.

"Will he really—" Kitty gave an exasperated sigh and moved closer on the squabs. She took her friend's gloved hand in her own. "Fiona," she whispered, "let us end this charade. I know. I know there's no friend."

Fiona's eyes filled with tears and she dabbed at them with her handkerchief. "How—"

"I guessed that first day when you told me the story." Kitty sighed. "I wished to respect your privacy. But my dear, this cannot go on."

"I—I know."

Kitty's fingers tightened. "My dear friend, shall I give you the money?"

"Kitty!" Fiona looked up in surprise. "I could not accept such a thing. I've no way to repay you."

Kitty pursed her lips. "Nonsense. I said nothing of repayment. Ginsfield would never miss it."

Fiona stared at her friend. How she wanted to say yes to this generous offer. To have this terrible thing over and done with. But much as she wanted to put this all behind her, she knew this was not the way. "Oh, Kitty, I wish I could. But I cannot. He will only come back. And it will go on and on."

"Then—"

A long shuddering sigh shivered through Fiona. "I shall have to tell him. I shall have to tell Dreyford the truth."

"Oh, yes!" said Kitty with a vehemence that surprised her friend. "Oh, my dear, I am so glad you came to this decision. It was my hope you would."

Fiona swallowed. "Why didn't you tell me before that you knew?"

The corners of Kitty's mouth lifted in the slightest of smiles. "I did not *know.* And that's why I didn't *ask.* Because if I *knew,* really knew, I would be honor bound to tell Dreyford."

Fiona did not quite comprehend the niceties of this kind of honor. But she did appreciate Kitty's friendship. "Thank you," she said. "Thank you for being my friend."

Kitty frowned. "*That* is my problem," she said. "I am friend to both of you. And my loyalties are sorely divided."

"Oh, Kitty, I did not mean to do that to you."

Kitty patted her arm. "It's all right now, my dear. You are going to do the right thing." She put a hand to her mouth. "You *are* going to tell him? You won't change your mind?"

"I won't change my mind."

Later, in the privacy of her room, Fiona paced. Back and forth, back and forth, she trod the expensive Persian carpet. Lady trailed at her heels for a while, then finally, unable to understand this peculiar behavior, curled up in a ball by the chaise and went to sleep.

I must tell him, Fiona thought, *but I must pick a good time, a time when he would not be upset—*

Her laughter rang out, a harsh bitter sound that startled the dog into wakefulness. She was being foolish, Fiona told herself. There was no good time to tell a man something like this.

She tried to imagine how he would react. Would he raise a dark eyebrow and laugh in disbelief? Or would he explode in a demonstration of the famed Dreyford temper?

She cast herself onto the chaise. Why didn't

Dreyford come home? This awful waiting would drive her mad. But no matter. Whatever his reaction, Dreyford must be told the truth.

Finally she washed her face and patted her hair into place. It couldn't hurt to look her best.

She got to her feet. She would go downstairs and work on her needlepoint. Anything would be better than waiting up here.

When she settled on the divan, the dog thrust her head into her lap. Fiona smoothed the silky hair. "You're lucky, all right," she whispered. "He cares about *you.*"

She was still sitting there, soothing herself by talking to the dog, when Dreyford came in. Her heart rose up in her throat at the sight of him. So dark, so handsome. Why must she love him so much?

"Good evening, my dear," he said.

"Good evening." The simple words wanted to stick in her throat. Should she tell him now? She moistened her lips, ready to begin.

And he smiled at her. That smile undermined all her determination and left her knees quivering.

Couldn't she have one more night? she asked herself. Was it too much to ask for one more night of happiness before it all came crashing down around her?

"And so, is your shelter about ready to open?" he inquired.

"Yes. The Hadleys are all moved in. And the animals have started coming in already." She managed a little laugh. "Ben has all the children alerted. Today they brought in two kittens and an abandoned dog."

His smile warmed her all the way through. Tomorrow he would cease smiling at her. She pushed tomorrow from her mind. She would not think about what might happen then. She would have her one perfect night. Smiling herself, she went to him and raised her face for his kiss.

• *Eleven* •

When Fiona went downstairs the next morning, the earl was gone and Berkins was waiting with a message that Caro Lamb had returned to the city. Fiona went first to see Caro.

"I have come to ask you a favor," she said, as soon as the greetings were over.

Caro looked up from her box of chocolates and smiled. "Of course, my dear. You know I would do anything for you. Ask away."

"As I told you in my letters, I have opened a shelter for homeless animals."

Caro examined a chocolate. "Yes, I remember a trifle about it."

"Well, something has happened," Fiona went on, leaning forward in her chair. "I may not be able to continue supporting it. And I thought perhaps you—"

Caro looked pained. "Oh, I assure you, I should help if I could, but William has become so stuffy lately."

"It would not take much," Fiona added hastily. "Perhaps the cost of one new gown a quarter."

Caro wrinkled her nose and selected a chocolate. "I dare not ask him for a penny. He simply flies up in the boughs. You understand, I'm sure."

Fiona slumped in her chair. She understood that she had been wrong about Caro Lamb. No tender heart beat beneath that delicate facade. This woman would not do anything to help anyone. She thought of no one but herself.

"But come," Caro cried, "and tell me all the latest *on dits.*"

Fiona sighed. She cared little for the ton these days—or its foolish gossip. "I'm afraid I must be going. Thank you for seeing me."

Caro got to her feet, consternation written on her face. "But, Fiona, you have not told me how Byron is. When did you see him last?"

Fiona bit back a sharp retort. "I saw him at Lady Jersey's last week. He looked well."

Caro frowned. "He did not look ill, or pining?"

"No, no. He was quite jovial—for him. Lady Jersey had put Lady Roxanne beside him."

Caro's nose wrinkled again. "That woman is no good."

"I know." Fiona moved toward the door. There was nothing she could do here. She did not want to talk to Caro anymore. Her so-called friend was every bit as shallow as Dreyford had said she was. "Good-bye, now."

Fiona told Huggins to take her next to Fleet Street. She went there every day and there was no point in avoiding the place now. Besides, she would rather face Lonigan there than in the drawing room on Grosvenor Square.

He came in midafternoon, ushered inside by a forewarned Mr. Hadley who closed the door carefully behind him. Lonigan's clothes were wrinkled and stained. His boots were worn down at the heels and spotted with mud. And his linen missed cleanliness by a wide margin. He looked like the seedy, run-down fortune hunter he actually was.

"So," he said, pulling up a straight chair and not wasting a minute. "Did ye get it?"

She sighed. It seemed impossible that once she had loved this man. How could she ever have believed in him?

He frowned. "I said, did ye get it?"

If only she had told Dreyford last night. It would be so much worse if Lonigan got to him first. "No, not yet."

"And why not, may I ask?" He glared at her across the battered table that served as a desk.

"I told you I need time." That was it, she thought, get him to give her more time, time to tell Dreyford about this. "It's difficult for me to come up with that much money right now."

Lonigan's eyes turned hard and avarice twisted his mouth, then his voice went deadly soft. "P'raps ye're right. A week ain't long. So I'll be generous." He paused and eyed her coldly. "One more week. And don't be failing me this time. Ye understand?"

She sighed. "Yes, I understand." She longed to tell him what she thought of him, a man who would blackmail a woman he had once purported to love. But she could not afford the luxury of anger, not until she had talked to Dreyford.

Lonigan got to his feet, his mouth stretched in an unpleasant smile. "I ain't gonna wait much longer," he said. "So ye'd best get busy."

"Yes," she murmured, swallowing hard. "I will do my very best."

And then he was gone. She sat there for a few minutes, deep in thought. Then she got up and went to look for Huggins. She was going home.

Once in the library she settled herself with her needlepoint. She would just keep herself calm and occupied until her husband arrived home. Dreyford was a reasonable man. Surely when she explained it to him— But her thoughts would carry her no further than that.

In and out the needle went. The clock in the corner ticked away the inexorable seconds and still Dreyford did not come. Her nerves were strung so taut that when Berkins appeared in the door, she started and gave herself a vicious stab with the needle.

"Yes, what is it?"

"A man in a carriage, milady. Says he was sent by Mr. Hadley."

Needlepoint forgotten, she leaped to her feet. "What has happened? What is wrong?"

Berkins frowned. "He said only that there was trouble."

"Trouble at the shelter?" She started toward the door. "I must go. Immediately."

Berkins trailed her down the hall. "But, milady, let me send for your carriage."

"No, no. There isn't time. I'll go with this man. You can send Huggins afterward. He can bring me home."

She hurried out the front door before he could say more. The nondescript man who was waiting said, "This way, milady. We'll be there afore you know it."

"Yes, yes." She allowed him to help her up the steps into the closed carriage. Just as she reached the top, she looked up. "Lon—"

She tried to turn, to go back, but the man gave her a quick shove and slammed the door behind her. She fell against the squabs near Lonigan's knees, and when she opened her mouth to scream, his hand closed over it.

He dragged her up onto the seat beside him. "Drive on!" he yelled.

She struggled against him, but to no avail. Finally, worn out, she subsided. "That's better," he said. "Ye be behaving yerself now and I'll let ye go."

As soon as he released her, she turned to him. "Why—why are you doing this?"

"I'm getting me a little nest egg." In the light of the carriage lamps his expression was almost jovial.

"I—I don't understand."

He laughed, and the sound chilled her blood. "Well, me dear, it's like this. I've me friends on Fleet Street. And I heard ye was out looking for

Brother Andrews." He laughed sardonically. "To think ye didn't trust yer own loving husband."

Anger gave her strength. "You're not my husband. And you never were. I'll wager you weren't pressed into the navy either. You were just through with me." She gasped. "You've probably been living in London the whole time."

"Ye ain't as believing as ye used to be," he said. "And it don't become ye. If ye'd just come up with a couple hundred pounds now and then, ye could have been spared all this."

She edged away from him. "What—what are you planning to do?"

"Why, I thought that was plain as day. I'm holding ye for ransom. And when yer loving hubby comes up with the blunt, then ye'll be let go."

"He won't stand for this!" she cried. "He'll track you down and kill you!"

Her outburst got no visible reaction from him. "I think not, me dear. He ain't gonna have no idee that I'm the one as has ye."

"But why— I was trying to get the money for you!"

"Sure an' ye was." The look in his eyes was decidedly unfriendly. "And ye was trying to find Brother Andrews, too."

"I only wanted to know the truth."

His gaze raked her over. "Well, now p'raps I'll tell ye the truth. Since it don't matter no more. Ye're right. Of course we was never married. Ye think I'd marry a poor relation? Not a chance. Not me."

A wave of relief swept over her. "Why don't you let me go?" she said. "I'll get Dreyford to pay you."

"Ha, ha. Ye're good at the jokes, me dear. Now ye jest sit still there and hush up. We've a way to go yet."

Drawing back into her corner of the coach, Fiona tried to think. Lonigan was wrong about one thing. There was someone who knew about him—Kitty. But how soon would Dreyford go to her? London was a big city. Even when they knew it was Lonigan, they would not know where to look. It seemed obvious that she could not count on them finding her. She must figure a way out of this herself.

Lonigan said he meant to let her go once he had the money. But would he really do that? Wouldn't it be simpler just to dispose of her? She shivered. If he were squeamish, he need not actually kill her. There were other ways, crueler than death, to dispose of a young woman in a city the size of London.

Her captor leaned back on the squabs, his eyes closed. She looked at the door. She might be able to get it open and throw herself out. But the carriage was traveling at a high speed and she was likely to be injured. Better to rest for now, to gather her strength for later. She closed her eyes.

When the carriage stopped several hours later, Lonigan straightened. "Well, me dear. Here we are."

She looked around, trying to mask her eagerness. There might be people outside. Perhaps she could get them to help her.

He turned. "This seems the easiest way." And he clipped her sharply on the chin.

When she came back to consciousness, she was in a room lying on a cot. Slowly she pushed herself upright. Her jaw was tender, and the room tilted a little at first, but she persisted and soon she could stand.

The room was empty. She crossed it and tried the door. It was locked, of course. She went to the window. Dusk had fallen, but outside was an innyard, ablaze with light. She pulled at the window, but it was fastened securely.

Slowly she made her way around the room, looking for something, anything, she could use as a weapon. She could not let Lonigan extract ransom money from Dreyford. She must find some way to escape him. And if he came back to this room for the night. . . . She shivered. She would die before she submitted to that man.

The dusk changed to complete darkness and gradually the bustle in the yard died down. Fiona peered out the window again. A shed roof below it would break her fall and allow her to slide to the earth below. But first she must find a way to get the window open.

She broke two fingernails prying at it, but to no effect. With a curse she turned away. There must be something—

The sounds of revelry floated up from below. Lonigan was no doubt down there, drinking, celebrating the good fortune he expected. And later—

Turning swiftly, she stumbled over the room's only chair, a rough wooden thing. That was it! Break it. Use part of it to smash the window.

She raised the chair over her head. But not on the floor. That would make too much noise. Instead she slammed it down on the cot. One leg broke off. She grabbed it. But wait— The noise of breaking glass might carry.

Reaching up under her gown, she grabbed a handful of petticoat. One good jerk ripped it loose. She wrapped it securely around the end of the chair leg, tying it in place.

Then, using it as a club, she broke the glass carefully out of the window. In the dim light it was hard to see, but she ran the club along the edges, trying to knock out all the jagged pieces. She worked fast, her hands sweaty. At any minute Lonigan might decide to return.

When the opening was clear, she waited a long, heart-stopping minute by the door, listening for the footsteps of someone who had come to investigate strange noises. But there was nothing but the echo of drunken laughter from below.

She turned away. It was time to go. She yanked the cover off the cot and rolled it into a ball, pushing it out the opening ahead of her. A long cold night awaited her if she managed to get away.

Though the window opening was small, she scrambled through it with only a few scratches. The drop to the ground wrenched her ankle and almost made her cry out in pain. But she bit down hard on her bottom lip, and scooping up the cover, limped off into the darkness, the sound of drunken voices fading behind her.

Fortunately for her the inn was set at the edge of a wood. She moved through the trees slowly. The pain in her ankle was receding a little and she wanted to hurry. But between the darkness and the pain, the going was slow.

She forced herself to keep walking. She should not stop too soon. Lonigan, fast talker that he was, was capable of mobilizing the whole inn to look for her. She pulled the cover around her shoulders and limped on, her breath coming harder.

She did not know how long she walked, but when finally she stopped, she had waded some distance down a creek and crossed to the other side. There she found a thicket and crawled in, pulling the brambles closed behind her.

In his London drawing room the Earl of Dreyford glowered at a frightened Ben. The earl had been in a vile mood all day. Someone had been circulating Roxanne's Fleet Street remark among the members of White's. He had barely escaped calling out some witless young fop. And then he'd arrived home to find his wife had gone rocketing off to that disreputable shelter, the cause of all his foul temper.

And now this—the stableboy had come panting in, cap in hand, to beg an audience.

"Well, what is it? What do you want?" the earl demanded, the Dreyford temper on the ascendancy.

"It's Her Ladyship," the boy stammered.

"She's at the shelter, boy. She can't talk to you now."

"Begging yer pardon, me lord, but she ain't. She ain't at the shelter."

The earl glared. "Boy, you must not contradict me."

The boy flushed a bright crimson, but he stood his ground. "But, me lord, she's took."

A distinct feeling of uneasiness hit the earl in his stomach. "Took? Whatever are you babbling about?"

"She's took!" Ben cried. "I seen it happen!"

Dreyford stared at him. Could he really mean— He drew the boy to a divan. "Sit down here and tell me exactly what you saw."

" 'Twas this afternoon—late. I seen the carriage come up. A man come to the door. Her Ladyship come running out."

Dreyford sighed. "I know all that. Berkins told me she was summoned to the shelter."

"But she weren't!" The boy was very insistent.

"How do you know this?"

"When she were getting in—it were a closed carriage—I saw the man. He shoved her in and he slammed the door after her. And the carriage took off, lickety-split."

"My God!" Dreyford was at last convinced. "Fiona! Abducted!"

Ben clutched his cap in nervous hands. "I think I knows where they went, me lord."

The earl grabbed him by the shoulders. "You what?"

The boy stared back at him bravely. "I followed the carriage, me lord. I thought to run for someone. But it were going too fast. So I hopped on the back."

"And—"

"It took the Dover Road. I dropped off when I were sure. That's why I'm only just back to tell you."

"The Dover Road." Dreyford got to his feet. "Ben, do you know any more? Have you any idea who did this thing?"

Ben hesitated. "I ain't sure. But I think I seen the man afore. On Fleet Street. He was with that flashy cove—the one what come here that day."

He knew instantly who the boy meant. "Lonigan!" Dreyford turned toward the door. "Don't worry, Ben. We'll get her back."

"Yes, me lord." The boy's lower lip trembled. "I hopes so, me lord."

It was well past midnight when Dreyford reined his stallion in and slid down at the inn. He had stopped at every establishment along the road and he was weary, and furious to boot. To think that this scoundrel had taken his wife. But he would suffer for it. Yes, indeed.

Everyone looked up when the door burst open and the irate lord came thundering in. And when they saw the look he gave Lonigan, the wise ones shrank away. Lonigan's eyes were not so glazed with drink that they couldn't recognize the turn fate had taken. Still, he tried to carry it off. "Why, 'tis the Earl of Dreyford. What be ye doing here?"

Dreyford strode across the room and lifted the drunken man by his coat front. "I have come for my wife. Where is she?"

"Yer—yer wife?" replied a stammering Lonigan, as the onlookers backed away.

"I do not intend to repeat myself." Dreyford shook him, as a terrier might a rat. "Where is she?" he demanded.

Apparently Lonigan realized that the jig was up. He crumpled and hung limp in the earl's grip. "She's—she's in the room at the top of the stairs. I ain't hurt her none."

"I should hope not." With a smile of complete satisfaction, Dreyford dealt the lout a hard left to the jaw and dropped him in a heap on the floor. Then he took the stairs two at a time and, not waiting to ask for a key, kicked the door in.

The room was empty. His eyes took in the battered chair and broken window, and a smile spread over his features. Fiona had escaped her captor. But where was she?

He went back down the stairs, more slowly than he had ascended them. Lonigan was gone, but Dreyford didn't care. He wanted only to find his wife, to hold her in his arms and tell her what this day had revealed to him. He loved her. He would no longer deny it to her. Or to himself.

• *Twelve* •

Early the next morning the singing of a wren woke Fiona. She was cold and stiff and hungry, but still she smiled. She had escaped Lonigan. He would not be likely to find her now.

Slowly she edged her way out of the thicket and took her bearings. It was best to follow the stream. Water always led to civilization.

Midmorning found her on the road back to London. In such light slippers her feet were soon bruised and sore. But home was still many weary hours away and somehow or other she meant to get there.

The sun rose to its highest and Fiona kept walking, putting one aching foot before the other. But as she walked, she thought.

She had built a false dream around a false man while all the time, right before her, was a real man, a man she could trust, could love. She did love Dreyford. She had never been more sure of anything in her entire life.

A sob rose in her throat. She loved a man who did not believe in love, who had told her he would never love. And now she had to confess to him this awful thing about herself. What would he say? What would he do?

Toward midafternoon the Earl of Dreyford sat in his library. An observer would not have recognized the well-known Corinthian with his disheveled hair, untidy cravat, and dusty boots. His eyes gazed unseeing at the Turner landscape above the mantel. From time to time he sighed, and the dog at his feet looked up at him with woeful eyes and wagged its tail.

He had not been to bed the night before, but had been waiting, sitting there ever since he'd returned from the Dover Road in the wee hours of the morning. He had scoured that road, all the way into the city, but there was just no sign of her.

He had sent men out to continue the search. They had apprehended Lonigan's confederate and Lonigan himself had fled. Surely Fiona would come home soon. There was nothing for it but to wait. But the hours dragged like long lonely years. "Where is she?" he asked the dog. "Why doesn't she come home?"

Wearily, he rose and went to stare out the window, into the sunlight-dappled courtyard where she had planted flowers. Where was she? And, more important, was she safe? In his mind he could see her so clearly—the thick chestnut hair he loved to stroke, the green eyes flecked with brown that flashed when she was angry, were warm when she was tender, the soft pink mouth, the warm pliant body that he had pressed so eagerly to his own.

Now, too late, he cursed the fact that he had never told her, never let her know what his feelings for her were. He rattled off a string of curses that would have made a coachman blanch. He was a damned fool for not recognizing his feelings sooner. For not letting her know.

He groaned aloud. "Fiona!" The dog came to him, pushing her cold nose into his hand. But she was scant comfort. She reminded him of the wife he had lost. Everything in this house reminded him. Good God! She had to come home. What would he do without her?

It was late afternoon when Fiona finally reached the house on Grosvenor Square. She climbed slowly down from the delivery wagon that had brought her the last few miles and thanked the kindhearted driver.

Outside the door, she shifted from one aching foot to the other. The hem of her skirt hung in tatters; a big rip left one sleeve flopping around her wrist. One of her slippers was losing its sole. And her face was streaked with dirt and sweat.

But none of that mattered. She was home at last.

And now Dreyford must be faced. She straightened her shoulders and lifted the knocker.

Berkins's mouth gaped. "Milady!" he cried, the picture of consternation. "We have been so worried about you. Are you all right? Shall I send for the physician?"

If only Dreyford cared this much, she thought. "I am fine," she assured the butler. "Just weary and footsore. I look much worse than I feel. Is the earl at home?"

"Yes, milady. He's in the library."

"Thank you." She pushed back her trailing hair and set off down the hall.

Dreyford was standing with his back to the door, staring into the courtyard.

The dog heard her and turned. With a joyful little yip, she ran to Fiona's feet. Blinking back her tears, Fiona bent to pat the dog's head.

But the earl did not turn. Did he already know what had happened? Did he mean not to speak to her at all? She moistened her lips and took a step into the room. "Dreyford."

He whirled. His face went as white as if he'd seen a spirit. "Fiona! Is it really you?"

"Yes." For a moment no more words would come. She wanted to run to him, but she did not dare. His eyes were so hard, his mouth so stern. How had she ever expected him to understand? "Did—did Lonigan send you a note about me, a ransom note?"

He nodded. "Yes, but have no concern about that. That has been taken care of."

Her knees trembling, she grasped the back of a nearby chair. "It has? How?"

He was still staring at her. "You may thank Ben," he said. "He saw you being shoved into the carriage. And he followed till he saw what road it took. Then I went looking for you."

"And you found Lonigan?"

His nod was grim. "Yes. I don't think he'll be bothering you again. If I'm not mistaken, he'll be far from London by now."

She wished to sit down, but she felt she must face him on her feet. She gripped the chair back harder. "Oh, Robert. I have so much to tell you."

He said nothing. He stood there, half a room away, waiting till she should condemn herself with her own words.

"It's about Lonigan," she said. "I knew Lonigan before. Long ago he came to Cousin Charles's. He was young and he was from my homeplace. He—he swept me off my feet. We ran away and were married. Or I thought we were married."

She saw the stiffening of his body, heard the quick intake of his breath, but still he said nothing. She forced herself to go on. "We went to London. And we were happy together. But one day he disappeared. When my money was gone, I had to return to Charles. Lonigan had been gone seven years when you came proposing marriage. Though I thought him probably dead, still I believed myself his wife. That is why I behaved so strangely afterward, denying you your rights."

She swallowed. "I should have told you. I did try to that day at Hinckley House. But you kissed me. And Charles— If I did not accept you, Charles meant to— But I should still have told you the truth."

She paused to steady herself, to pull her thoughts together. "I believed Lonigan was dead. Truly I did. And then he showed up. First at the shelter. And then that day at the house. He asked me for money—a couple hundred pounds. Otherwise he meant to tell you we were married. I put him off, saying I needed time." She sighed. "Seeing him then, seeing what he was, I suspected he had duped me, that there had been no legal marriage. So I went looking for the preacher, Brother Andrews. We did not find him, of course. I know now there was no marriage." She swallowed. "And I should tell you, I asked Kitty to help me."

His frown deepened. "Oh, please," she hurried on, "you must not be angry at Kitty. She did not know the whole story. Till the day before yesterday. When I decided to tell you the truth."

Finally he spoke, his voice deep, his words like a pronouncement of doom. "But you did not tell me."

The dog whimpered and slunk under the divan.

Fiona pulled herself more erect. "No. And that was my first mistake. I didn't tell you because I wanted to have one last happy night with you. And then yesterday, when the man came saying there was trouble at the shelter, I ran out—not thinking."

He took two steps toward her. "And Lonigan abducted you."

"Yes."

He stared at her for a long terrifying moment, and then he crossed the space between them and crushed her to him. He kissed the breath from her body. When he released her mouth, her knees had given way. But she found herself, inexplicably, caught up in his arms. He crossed the room to the divan, where he gently put her down, then settled himself beside her.

This gentleness of his confused her. He was looking so concerned, like a man who really cared about his wife. Was he going to react as he had that night in the carriage? She turned in his arms till she could see his face. "You are not angry with me?"

He dropped a kiss on her forehead. "I am outraged," he said, but his expression belied his words. "But I believe I can understand why you did not tell me the truth that day at Hinckley's. You truly believed the man dead."

His smile was so tender. Could she be dreaming all this? Could she still be in the thicket, dreaming along the Dover Road?

The dog scrambled out from under the divan and thrust her head into Fiona's lap. Absently, Fiona stroked Lady's soft ears. If she were dreaming, would she dream about the dog?

She lay her cheek against her husband's chest and sighed. "I know you do not love me. But I must tell you, Robert. I—I love you."

She heard his exclamation, but she dared not look up into his face. "I am sorry, Robert. But truly, I cannot help it. You know love is important to me."

There was a long silence while she waited, but he said nothing. Finally she could stand it no longer. "You—you said you had something to tell me."

"Yes, I have." His voice seemed husky. "It's

about our marriage. I only hope you will not be angry with me."

"I no longer care about my homeplace," she hastened to tell him. "Whatever your reasons for marrying me you have always been good to me."

He sighed. "Still, I must tell you the truth. I did not marry you for that piece of Irish land as you supposed I did."

Still she dared not look at him. "Then, why?"

His fingers moved, softly, gently, on her hair. "When I was young, very young, I loved a girl. Katie Howard was her name. She looked very much like you look. She died quite young. When you came into Charles's library that day, I thought for a moment that she had come back to me."

She looked up at him. "So that is why you looked so startled."

"Yes. So you see, the land was really unimportant to me. I married you because you looked like my Katie. And I could not bear the thought of that fat pig putting his hands on you. I did not tell you that, of course. I preferred to let you think otherwise."

He kissed her forehead. "But I soon grew to care for you for yourself. You are quite lovable, you know. Except when you take a stand."

She had been so unfair to him. "Yes, well, it appears that I was wrong about that, too. Caro Lamb is not the person I thought her."

"Indeed." His expression grew whimsical. "And how did you discover this?"

"I asked her for help with the shelter."

He laughed and drew her closer. "And she gave you nothing but excuses."

"Yes," she agreed. "But I still do not think her as bad as your Roxanne."

"Nor I. Not really. But, Fiona, she is not *my* Roxanne. I will be truthful with you about this, too. When we married, I fully meant to continue my liaison with her. But I went to her only once. It was one of those first nights after we returned to the city." He chuckled. "One of those nights when we had so much trouble with the door. I went to her, but I did not stay. Because I found I wanted to be with you. I believe I loved you even then. Though of course I did not know it."

She stared up at him. "But, Robert, how can you love me? You do not believe in love. You told me yourself that love is foolish. That you would never love anyone."

He grinned. "I was the foolish one, pet. Even then I loved you."

She kissed his chin. "Kitty said—"

He kissed her ear. "What did Kitty say?"

"She said you are capable of great love."

"She knew about Katie. All these years she has kept my secret."

Tenderly, she touched his cheek. "I knew I was right to want her for my friend. She will be very pleased at our happiness."

"No more than I, my love. No more than I."

Laughter bubbled up in her. It was true, really true. Robert loved her. "I still cannot believe it. You, the man who said love was for girls fresh out of the nursery."

He got to his feet and lifted her into his arms. The dog, her tail wagging, fell into place at his heels. "On the matter of love," he said softly, "I have quite changed my mind."

With his heart beating steadily beneath her ear, Fiona smiled. There in his arms she was safe. There, at last she had found her homeplace.

He carried her down the hall to where the beaming butler stood. "Berkins," he said, "we are not at home to visitors. See that we are not disturbed. We shall be having a serious discussion on the nature of love. And I expect it to last for some time."

"Yes, milord."

In the shadows by the far door, Ben wiped the happy tears from his cheeks. He'd just wanted to make sure she was safe and sound, the lady who'd been so good to him. But there was no cause to worry. The master would take care of her now. He loved her too.